# Uncompromising

## Book TWO in the
## "Casts of Silver" Series

# K.J. ROWE

Ark House Press
PO Box 1722, Port Orchard, WA 98366 USA
PO Box 1321, Mona Vale NSW 1660 Australia
PO Box 318 334, West Harbour, Auckland 0661 New Zealand
arkhousepress.com

Cataloguing in Publication Data:
Title: Uncompromising
ISBN: 978-0-6453370-7-5 (pbk)
Subjects: Fiction
Other Authors/Contributors: Rowe, K.J.

Design by initiateagency.com

*"Trust in the Lord with all your heart, and lean not on your own understanding; In all your ways acknowledge Him, and He shall direct your paths."*
Proverbs 3:5–6 NKJV

# ACKNOWLEDGEMENTS

First, I would like to thank the Lord God above for inspiring me to write this series. For guiding me and my testimony through the pages of these books to show the goodness of God and power of prayer in all circumstances.

Iola Goulton of Christian Editing Services who wove her gifted pen over these words to shape it into life. Your insights and humour made the process not only educational – no one ever stops learning – but fun! Thankyou!

Nicole Danswan of Initiate Media for bringing Dylan (and Lexi) to life through the cover art of the series thus far. To actualize my visions…I need to send you chocolate! Thankyou!

The team at Ark House for welcoming me and putting my work together. You've made a dream possible. Thankyou!

My incredible proof readers (from book 1 also) Nova, Karen O, Karen R & Amanda, thankyou for being a fresh set of eyes over my work. To plough through early drafts is not an easy feat. You ladies are an incredible blessing in my life! Thankyou!

# ONE

With clenched fists, Dylan Saunders thrust his arms in the late September air and roared above the buzzing siren of The Valley Football ground. Five years of disappointments were over, and the cup was theirs!

Out of breath, he dropped to his knees and let his arms fall limp to his sides while he tilted his head back and replenished his lungs with the salty sea air. The Tigers club song blasted over the oval, filled him with euphoria while horn blasts from the car park and cheers from the boundary line chorused alongside.

"Dylan!"

With a quick scan of the crowds, Dylan's smile amped up and he got to his feet. Mum and his uncle leaned over the boundary fence, waving team scarves.

"Uncle Shane!" Dylan gave his hand a firm shake. "I wasn't expecting to see you!"

"Your dad would have been proud, my boy! Twenty-three and holding a Grand Final medallion for his club…"

Dylan laughed. "Only just beat him. He was twenty-four when you blokes won your first, right?"

"That's right." Uncle Shane dipped his head before hanging the Tigers scarf around his neck once more. "Well, he was twenty-four. I was twenty-one," he added with a wink.

Dylan embraced his Mum, swallowing the lump that formed in his throat at the mention of Dad's playing days with Uncle Shane. Dylan often prayed the same would happen for him with his own brother, though that idea was becoming less and less likely with Jack's disinterest in anything he did.

"Thanks for coming, Mum." She smiled back at him, her eyes brimming with tears. "Wouldn't have missed it sweetie. I'm sorry Jack couldn't make it."

Dylan acknowledged Jack's absence with a dismissive nod and released Mum. He hadn't expected Jack to turn up.

Dylan could hear his teammates calling him over the celebrations taking place around the oval, but he hadn't seen his uncle in over a year. He signaled five minutes to his teammates. "So you in town long, Uncle Shane?"

"I'll fly home Monday. Now, go celebrate with your friends. We can catch up tomorrow."

"Great. I'll look froward to it." Dylan turned and sprinted across the ground to catch his teammates, thrilled Mum and Uncle Shane had seen the game and Shane was in town for the weekend. He caught up with the team just in time and joined in as they charged Andrew Bryson, their captain, and lifted him onto their shoulders like a feather.

The atmosphere was electric and with one arm helping to hold up his Captain, Dylan played up to the ongoing antics from the boundary line crowds. Once they passed through the doors into the clubrooms, and Andrew back on his feet, they sung the club's anthem as loud as they could. Dylan's lungs burned with effort and his head swam, but it was a feeling like no other. Local reporters surrounded their huddle with TV cameras and microphones, but he paid them no attention. This day was a long time coming, and he was going to drink in every moment with his teammates.

"To the Beachside!" Andrew shouted as they sang the last word of their anthem, and his shout was echoed like a war cry from the rest of the team before another round of violent back-slapping sent Dylan stumbling into a reporter. He righted himself and helped the surprised young woman up, then joined the mass exodus leaving the clubrooms.

After a quick stop at home to shower and change, Dylan pulled his Harley Davidson motorbike up outside the Beachside Hotel, kicked out the stand and unclipped his helmet. The sidewalks bustled with people enjoying the clear balmy night. Conversations battled the drone from the constant stream of traffic along The Valley main street beside him. Seagulls hovered, hoping for one more crumb from the alfresco diners. Among the noise, Dylan felt peaceful. The day had been surreal, and he wanted to hold onto each moment.

"Saunders. Come on, bro. Party is inside!" Andrew called out to him.

His captain's comment brought a smile to Dylan's face as he looked over his shoulder. A number of his teammates were striding the sidewalk towards him, drinks in hand and female companions by their sides.

"Your bike won't disappear. Let's go." Andrew gestured for Dylan to join them inside.

Dylan chuckled. They knew he loved his bike, but he sensed they spoke from jealousy. "I'm right behind you."

The Beachside was packed. Inside, red and white dotted the bar, the dining room, the alfresco patio, and the beer garden. Everyone in The Valley was celebrating with them. Dylan scanned the room for faces he wanted to see, thankful for his six feet and five inches in height. Spying his teammates in the beer garden, he wove his way through the crowded hotel to join them.

"Here he is." Nick rose from his bar stool as Dylan approached. "The man who kicked the winning goal. We're honored to have you join our humble party."

Dylan looked away as he dragged a bar stool over to their table, not wanting the grin on his face to appear cocky. He composed himself and looked back at his friend. "Thanks, Nick, but I can't take all the credit. It was one hell of a team effort."

"How were you not injured when that guy tripped you up in the third quarter?" Lexi asked.

Dylan rolled his shoulder out and wondered the same. He'd fallen hard, but it felt fine. He gave her a wink. "Not sure, Lex, but I feel great."

"You'll be feeling it tomorrow." Nick said.

Trent laughed, toasting Nick's comment, "and I'm sure by the sound of your voice right now...you'd better carry a notepad around with you tomorrow in case you want something."

"And *I'm* sure," Hope rose from her seat. "After he finally gets that butt on the dance floor –"

"Hey hey hey." Dylan held his hands up, then gestured to himself. "This body doesn't dance for just anybody …"

Playful calls of challenge echoed around the table at his words. Lexi's eyes grazed his as she stood to join Hope, and he knew her thoughts mirrored his own. Just last weekend, he'd danced with her—a dance that had changed everything for them.

A heavy body bumped into him, and he caught himself against the table.

"Hey, kids. What's happening?" asked Josh Anderson, Dylan's teammate. He glanced over the table at Hope, who was shrugging off her jacket while whispering something to Lexi. Hope had her eye on Josh and hadn't been shy about showing her interest, but Josh was more traditional and found a forward woman intimidating. It had taken a number of talks and jibes to get Josh to call her, and tonight was meant to be their first date.

"There's not much celebrating going on here." Josh's beer lapped over the glass as he nudged Dylan. "How about we liven this party up a little?"

"Oh, we're going to." Hope took Lexi's hand and dragged her towards the dance floor. "You coming?"

Josh watched as Hope disappeared into the crowd but didn't move.

Dylan cleared his throat. "I think that was your cue, champ." He shook his head, and the rest of the boys rolled their eyes in return.

"It was a good game, wasn't it?" Josh kept watching Hope as he fumbled for the table with his empty glass. The glass bumped the table, and Josh flicked a glance at them and pushed it onto the table. "Here's hoping next year will be just as good. Gotta run."

Josh left their table and hurried after the girls. Nick chuckled.

"He's hungry.' Nick sat back in his chair.

Trent nodded and refilled his glass with water from the table. "Why aren't you joining them?"

Dylan lifted a shoulder. "I'm still in the relaxing part of the evening." He wanted to join Lexi on the dance floor, but he also wanted to spend time celebrating and relaxing with his teammates. Lexi and the dance floor were far from relaxing.

"How are things between you guys?" Trent asked, tone cautious.

Dylan tipped the chip bowl towards him and picked at the few remaining crumbs. Trent's ability to see past pretense made it hard to hide anything.

"Hard to say. I tried to talk with her at Hope's movie night, but we were … interrupted." Dylan pushed the bowl away from him, blowing his breath out. "Wouldn't know what to say to her anyway even if another moment presented itself."

"Come on, man. It's simple. You tell her how you've been keen on her for a while, she tells you how she had no idea, you fall into each other's arms, and the rest is happily ever after. What's so hard?" Nick took a long sip of his water as Trent chuckled into his drink.

Dylan returned Nick's steady gaze and raised his eyebrows, hiding his irritation at Nick's cavalier attitude. "Nick, so much of what you said is just—" Dylan caught himself.

Lexi and Hope reappeared at their table, eyes shining and their skin glistening with sweat. He placed his drink back on the table, pulse jumping at the unexpected sight of Lexi. "Back already?"

"You boys coming?" Hope asked. "Or is your big night celebrating going to be sitting here, eating chips?"

While Trent and Nick began to rebut Hope's protest, Dylan tuned out. Lexi had her hair piled on top of her head showing off her neck and the curves of her collarbone. What held him back?

"What are we all still doing here?" Josh asked with tried patience, a fresh beer in hand, and hair curling on his sweat-slickened forehead. "You boys have to be celebrating in the most boring way! Do I have to remind you big fella, we've just won a grand final? Let's go."

Dylan dropped his gaze from Lexi, allowing his teammate to jostle him.

"We're celebrating how we want to celebrate." Nick said, his tone indifferent.

Josh laughed. "Righto, grandpa. Well, you'll know where to find us when you've finished your nap."

The beer garden doors opened again. People came and went, filling the open air with a familiar rock anthem. Hope bounced on the spot. "Oh, I love this song!" she shouted, her blond bob settling after a second bounce. "Come on, guys. The floor's calling."

"Sure you're not coming?" Lexi asked.

Sensing the question was directed at him, Dylan shifted his gaze back to her. Her blue eyes sparkled as usual, but the way she caught her bottom lip in her teeth revealed the worry within the question. His coolness faltered. Something big had changed in their friendship over the last week, and he wasn't used to it. One thing he knew was that he needed to be careful.

"I'd take that has a no," Josh draped his arms around Hope and Lexi. "Enjoy your relaxing, boys."

Dylan swiveled on his seat to watch the trio turn to leave the beer garden. Their laughter goaded him, but it was the smug grin Josh flashed back as he opened the door, that sealed the deal.

"Come on, mate. Why aren't you joining them?" Trent asked after the door shut behind them, muffling the raucous beyond.

Dylan stood, shrugged off his jacket, then glanced at Nick and Trent.

"Who said I wasn't?"

# TWO

A heavy scent of cigarettes and cloying perfumes greeted Dylan as he pushed through the heavy glass doors back into the hotel and into the deafening bass of the cover band. He glanced over the crowds towards the stage, searching the swaying multitudes for that familiar shade of red.

"Hey, you've decided to join us after all." Lexi shouted from behind him.

Dylan turned. Lexi moved to the music, holding what looked like iced tea, her trademark drink.

"I thought you didn't dance for just anybody." She stepped forward to shout over the music.

She held the straw of her drink between her teeth, which kept his attention on her mouth. Funny how things could change so dramatically in such a short space of time.

"I don't." He moved his gaze to her eyes, enjoying the way the color heightened in her cheeks. Her eyes shimmered back at him like reflections in a kaleidoscope. An unwanted presence materialized beside him and he turned slowly to view the intruder, though he was sure he already knew who it was.

"So what are we up to, kids?" Nick asked, feigning innocence.

Dylan eyeballed Nick, hoping telepathy conveyed his thoughts.

"Hey guys. You've finally joined us." Hope shouted nearby.

Nick turned to face Hope as she joined them, breaking the standoff. Josh had his arm around her waist. If only he could consider being so bold. "I told you'd I'd make an appearance."

"Let's see if you can make it a few more feet to the dance floor then, big fella." Josh's eyes darted to Lexi and back again, lingering a moment to ensure Dylan caught the hint before guiding Hope towards the dance floor, Nick trailing behind.

Dylan chuckled as they wandered off, and he turned his attention back to Lexi. The haphazard lighting in the room illuminated her face as she watched the band performing. He took a step towards her to ask for a dance but paused when a beam of light highlighted the marks on her face. She'd tried to cover yellow-brown hues shadowing her eye and cheek with make-up, but the harsh lighting in the bar gave her away.

Maybe it was too soon. She'd only just come out of an abusive relationship. Almost kissing her last night at Hope's movie marathon had been a mistake. He'd only meant to talk to her and encourage her. He'd never been so thankful to be interrupted. Lexi was vulnerable. She needed her friend, not a proposition. He caught his words in time, bypassed her searching eyes and looked past her as he spoke.

"So, Hope and Josh aye?"

Was that the best he could come up with? He'd helped set them up, so why would he be surprised? He mentally punched himself in the face. Small talk was not his strength.

"Yeah. She told me earlier that she had a date with him teed up for tonight," Lexi said.

"You guys came here together, didn't you? Dylan asked.

"Yeah."

"How are you getting home tonight?"

"I brought my Jeep." Lexi dangled the keys before him.

"Ah." Dylan nodded as she took another suck of her drink, drawing his attention to her mouth again. He rubbed the back of his neck and chuckled, dropping his gaze he tried to think of something to say, and not think about what it would taste like to kiss those glossy lips.

"Dylannn!"

The war-like-cry sounding above the band as Dylan's teammates pushed through the crowded bar towards him. He stepped in front of Lexi so they didn't bowl her over in their enthusiasm, and planted himself in readiness for the onslaught. It came like a tidal wave and he doubled back, just managing to keep his feet as he stumbled amongst the rabble. Lexi's palms pressed into his back and she gave an excited giggle. Then her palms were gone, and she stepped out from behind him and wove her way towards the dance floor.

His teammate's shouts, cheers and dares drew him back to why he was at the bar tonight in the first place.

To celebrate. And did they celebrate. Hours later, hoarse from singing along with the band, Dylan slouched over a glass of water in the cool beer garden. His white shirt was covered with wine spills and random comments scrawled by his teammates and friends using pens found behind the bar, and he had a splitting headache. Somewhere during the celebrating, his friends had slipped away.

"Hey, Saunders."

Andrew sat down heavily opposite him and placed his beer on the bar table. He looked as disheveled as Dylan imaged himself to look, and the man's usual impeccably styled hair … well, Dylan wished he had a camera. A shot of this would provide him with a lot of leverage, should he ever need any.

"Hey." Dylan straightened his spine and took in a long breath.

"What a day huh?" Andrew sounded sleepy.

"Surreal."

"I see you're on the hard stuff there." Andrew gestured to the glass of water Dylan was absentmindedly passing from hand to hand. Dylan drained the glass, wishing the jackhammer in his head would cease. "Aren't I always?"

"You know we have a barbecue lunch tomorrow at the club, right?" Andrew asked.

"Yeah." Dylan looked over his glass at the club captain. The man had an agenda behind his question, but what?

Andrew rolled out his shoulder. "So we'll see you there?"

"Yeah." Dylan gave a slow nod.

"Good. Don't be late."

His captain rose without another word and left the beer garden. Dylan sat back in his seat as a gentle breeze blew in from the sea. The air filled with the imminent scent of summer.

He knew what tomorrow's barbecue was about. They were going to ask him to be team captain.

# THREE

Dylan shuffled along the wooden floor towards the kitchen, rubbing a hand over his bare chest. So this was what being hit by a bus felt like. He was completely drained after yesterday's physical exertions and emotional highs. He yawned, moving from his room to the kitchen for food on auto-pilot, drawn by the scent of bacon and eggs. His younger brother was already seated at the small oval dining table, eating the breakfast he'd made only for himself. He dipped his head in greeting and continued to the fridge.

"You were home late." Jack said, reproach tainting his words.

Dylan looked back at Jack and raised an eyebrow. "What's the rule in this house?" His words rasped out of his dry mouth. Jack rolled his eyes and took another bite of his toast, spilling bacon and eggs back onto the plate. "No talking with your mouth full."

Dylan ignored Jack's attitude and selected a grape juice from the fridge before moving slowly to the table and lowered himself into a seat. Every muscle in his body protested. If it wasn't for the coach wanting all the team members at the clubhouse for a that quiet barbecue lunch, he'd have stayed in bed. Or gone for a massage.

"Morning, boys."

Dylan winced at Mum's singsong voice piercing the quiet of the kitchen. He lifted a hand in greeting without turning and sipped his juice. It was uncharacteristic for Mum to be so happy in the morning. What was up? She took out a box of cereal and served herself breakfast.

"How was everything here last night?" Dylan took another sip of his drink, hoping the thick syrupy liquid would soothe his throat.

Jack stood, scraping his chair along the wooden floor. "Everything was fine. The place doesn't fall apart when you're not around, you know. Just because you're four years older than me, doesn't make you the boss."

Jack stalked from the room. Dylan pushed his brothers chair back under the table and turned a questioning gaze to his mother. She had paled and her chirpy morning aura had vanished.

"You alright?" he asked.

"Fine sweetie." She waved a hand. "Tell me about your big day yesterday."

"It was great." He told her what Andrew had said at the pub. She mm'd as if she was listening, but he sensed her mind was elsewhere. "Mum?"

A door slammed, and she jumped. Jack's old Datsun started up and chugged down the driveway. When her eyes flicked to his, they were shuttered and her expression neutral.

"I'm sorry, darling. Jack insisted on going out to a party last night, which I didn't want him to go to. He went anyway, and was brought home by the police—"

"The police?"

She and took her bowl to the sink, mumbling an answer Dylan didn't catch. He got up and followed her. "What'd you say?"

When she didn't answer, Dylan stilled her hands from the furious cleaning of the dishes in the sink, and gentled. "Mum, what happened last night?"

She let out a heavy sigh and tilted her head back, closing her eyes. "He doesn't listen to me. I've warned him not to hang around with those people, but it's like I'm not even here."

"So what happened?

She rubbed a hand over her face, then hugged herself.

"Well, I may have had something to drink after he left. I may have been a little tipsy when the police turned up to deliver him home, and I may have had a little lecture from Mr. Policeman about responsible parenting. After he left, I had a yelling match with Jack to finish the evening. So I decided to have another drink. Or three."

Dylan stepped back and leant against the counter, crossing his arms. He took a deep breath and sent a quick prayer up to God for Jack. "Is Jack in trouble?"

"The police suspect Jack is involved in some local crimes. They asked where he'd been at certain times. But I have no idea where he is half the time, so I wasn't much help."

"What sort of crimes?"

Mum fiddled with the latch on her wrist watch. "They think he's stolen some things and damaged some property. I didn't ask details … at least, I don't remember asking."

"Why didn't you call me?" Dylan asked, his mind whirling with thoughts of what Jack might have done.

Mum's eyes flashed. "I'm the parent here. Not you."

"I'm not say—"

"Just go." She turned back to the kitchen sink. The morning sun highlighted the strain lines around her mouth and the grey roots peeking through her colored blond hair.

As much as he wanted to say, he had an undeniable feeling that now was the time to hold his tongue. Anger stirred within him. Why did Jack push her?

They had to talk. Preferably before dinner with Uncle Shane. He'd grab Jack as soon as he got home. Whenever that would be.

* * *

Dylan pulled his helmet off, sat it on the handlebars, and pinched the bridge of his nose. Riding the Harley after a big night was not a good idea. The roar of the engine did nothing for the evil headache keeping him company, and he sat still for a long moment, hoping the needling in his skull would subside.

"Hey hey hey!" Josh called from across the car park.

Dylan turned slowly. "Why are you so spritely?"

"Why aren't you?" Josh laid a few heavy raps on Dylan's back.

He groaned at the unexpected barrage, holding a hand up for peace. Josh took a few steps back, and Dylan moved slowly off his bike. "I woke up feeling like I'd been hit by a bus. If I had my way, I'd still be in bed. Not trying to be sociable at a BBQ."

"Ah well, man up."

Josh was too sprightly. It was the morning after a big game, which had been followed by an evening of celebrating. Dylan glanced at him as they headed towards the clubrooms. There was something he wasn't saying.

"How'd last night go? Can we say you're now a spoken-for man?" Dylan asked.

Josh chuckled as he roughed up his mop of hair. The slight reddening of his cheeks brought a grin to Dylan face. "You sly dog."

"What about you?" Josh asked. "I saw you making a move…finally."

"Let's just say I've decided to hold off that one for the moment."

Josh stepped in front of him, and Dylan halted. Questions marked Josh's features, and Dylan sighed. Cars were pulling into the car park and their teammates were slowly filing into the clubrooms. "It's not the right time, mate. I don't want to rush things … or her."

"That wasn't the impression I was getti—"

"Things change, Josh." Maybe he shouldn't have confided in Josh about his changed feelings towards Lexi. He glanced towards the clubrooms. And he had other things to worry about. Whatever was going to happen in the clubrooms. And what he was going to go home to afterwards. The two were counter balanced. He had to think of them first.

"Sorry, Josh," Dylan said. "I probably spoke out a little too quickly in that area—it's been a crazy week, as you know. Lex and I will work things out in time, but we're here for a club barbecue and meeting. We better get inside before we get called in."

"No worries, D. I've got your back." Josh rapped Dylan on the shoulder and turned back towards the clubroom again, just as

Andrew appeared in the doorway. "Meeting's inside, fellas. Let's go," Andrew called.

Dylan glanced at his waiting captain, chuckling to himself. Andrew's well-manicured appearance was securely back in place.

"Thanks, Josh." Dylan nodded towards the clubrooms. "Let's get this big-game-wrap-up barbecue out of the way. I want to go home and back to bed."

# FOUR

The clubrooms were bright with midday sun, and clearly hadn't been visited by the cleaners since the before yesterday's big game.

Dylan pulled up a seat up by the floor-to-ceiling windows overlooking the Tigers' home ground and sat with his back against the window. The radiating warmth soothed his tired body. He yawned and accepted the glass of water Max Mason handed him .

"How's it going, big fella?"

Max, the surprisingly intelligent club clown, straddled the seat he'd swung around and sipped from his own glass of water. His usual glowing olive complexion had a slight grey tinge. "You look about how I feel."

"I think we're all a little under the weather this morning."

"All except Josh."

"Except me what?" Josh took the seat on Dylan's other side, and crossed his ankles over the table in front of them. There was a mischievous glint in his eyes that sold him out as he looked between Dylan and Max. He looked like a toddler on Christmas morning.

"Double win yesterday, I hear." Max leaned over Dylan and rapped Josh's thigh. "She's cute. Nice work."

Dylan turned his attention towards the front of the room where Andrew and the club president, Michael Smith, were standing. He didn't want to hear Max's comments about Hope, nor get pulled into Max's sly way of eliciting gossip. Dylan liked the guy but didn't seek his company outside the club.

Max elbowed Dylan in the side. "Did you hear talent scouts were at the game yesterday? Reckon they'll be after your number."

A grin tugged on Dylan's mouth. Playing AFL was a pipe dream.

Max leaned in, his voice hushed. "Think about it. What if a club did contact you? You'd be travelling the country, earning megabucks, be on TV every week … Imagine the girls you'd have to pick from."

Dylan shook his head and turned his attention back to the stage. There was only one girl he was interested in—Lexi—and he was hardly good enough to play big time.

Andrew and Michael flicked glances in his direction as the rest of the team made their way inside, and Dylan set his thoughts heavenward. Whatever the outcome of todays' meeting and barbecue, he would trust God had it covered.

"Welcome, Tigers," Michael said. "Thank you all for turning out today, especially you Gil. How is that collarbone?"

"Snapped clean through." Gil McGuire said with pride, gesturing gestured to his arm in a sling. His screaming mark of the football yesterday, had come with the hefty price of a broken collarbone, but he wore it like a trophy.

"You all played extremely well yesterday, boys," Andrew said. "I'm thrilled to be finishing my football career on a high, but I won't step down unless I can be sure the team will be led strongly after I'm gone. Which leads to why Michael and I have asked you all bring your sad-and-sorry worn-out bodies in this morning."

"We can't all look as good as you, Bryson."

"It starts with a simple shower, Carl …"

Dylan leaned forward in his seat, chuckling as Andrew left the obvious suggestion hanging. The warming rays of the sun made him sleepy, and he warred with his eyelids to stay open after every blink. Thankfully, Michael called the team to order.

As the scent of sausages and hamburgers cooking outside on the barbecue wove their way into the club house, Dylan found his mind wandering. All he'd had for breakfast was a grape juice, and his empty stomach and pounding headache were combining to make him feel nauseous.

"… Dylan Saunders!"

The room erupted with applause. Dylan sat up fast and looked around to meet the gazes of his teammates as they cheered. He glanced between Josh and Max then rose to his feet and made his way around the tables, and towards the stage. Even though he'd tuned out the intros, he knew why he was being called up.

"Fellas." Dylan stepped onto the stage and shook Michael then Andrew by the hand. How was he going to answer the question they were about to ask? He still wasn't one hundred per cent sure. "Dylan, it's no secret, so well get straight to the point."

Michael glanced around the room. "We, as a board and as a team, want you to step up and lead this premiership team next year." Michael's voice got louder as he spoke, and the room was filled with deafening cheers and kudos of encouragement for Dylan to accept the role. Michael's heavy hand clamped on his shoulder, pressing him for a response.

Dylan rubbed the back of his neck as the applause settled. Anticipation filled the air.

"D." Andrew moved to stand beside Michael, hand outstretched. "Man, she's all yours. Take her into the glory years ahead."

More cheers. More catcalls. More praises rang out.

Lexi's words echoed through his mind: "God would never ask you to do something if it would negatively impact your family."

Andrew's steady hand remained in front of him, his hazel eyes locked on his.

A steady chant rose throughout the room. Dylan, Dylan, Dylan. His teammates rapped on tables and raised their glasses, all egging him on to take the role.

Dylan thought of Jack and Mum and sent a prayer up to God that this was His will, then reached out and clasped Andrew's hand.

"Will be my pleasure."

And truly, it would be.

# FIVE

Dylan laughed at Hope's animated squeal beside him in the minibus he was driving.

"There they are, there they are!" Hope pointed out her window, bouncing in the seat beside him, "Put your foot down!"

"I see 'em, I see 'em!" Dylan concentrated on the road ahead and keeping the minibus steady at sixty kilometers per hour. "Did you see where they went?"

"They've turned down Roberts Avenue." Hope said.

They were headed for the supermarket. Which meant Dylan and Hope's team were only just in front, because the supermarket challenge didn't take long. He flicked a glance in the rearview mirror to see their team trying to work out the next clue.

"Anybody got it worked out yet?" Dylan called out, eager to maintain their lead.

Murmurs of confusion grew louder behind him and Dylan glanced across at Hope. "Any ideas?"

She shrugged before turning to face the back of the bus. "C'mon guys, let's go. Nat, can you read the clue out again?"

Dylan glanced in the mirror again as the young girl held up the list of clues. Car rally evenings were always good fun. Nerve racking, but good fun.

"Get a clearer perspective while readying for the journey." Nat called out in a strong loud voice.

As the youth discussed the clue, Dylan took in the sights of The Valley at dusk. The businesses were closed, and the night-life was gearing up. Cars lined the strip outside the pubs and restaurants while happy laughter could be heard floating on the evening air. He loved this time of the day. The night was warm and—"It's a fuel station." Cody shouted from the back of the bus, breaking Dylan's reflections. "We have to get to a fuel station and clean somebodies car windows!"

Dylan changed down a gear and took the next left turn, thankful for a green arrow that appeared to be waiting for them as they approached the intersection. The youth all started talking at once.

"Hurry. Hurry, they're going to catch us!" Laura shouted.

"There's a petrol station on the right," Ryan called.

"We'll have to wait to turn across the traffic if we take that one. There another one further up on the left," Dylan called back. "Stay in your seats, guys."

"Just get us to the closest one. Quick." Chloe said.

Dylan laughed as he glanced at the youth in his rearview mirror, "Who's driving this bus?"

"Hurry!" They all shouted in unison.

Not two minutes later, Dylan pulled the minibus up at a fuel station and opened the doors. The youth scrambled out, keen to fulfil the challenge. He jumped down from his seat and leaned against the bus to watch on. The youth were eager to complete the challenges, but he hoped they also understood the message of the Random Acts of Kindness car rally, that it wasn't just a matter of being the fastest back to Pastor Walker's home.

"One more to go after this." Hope came to stand beside him. "Call me silly, but I can't work this one out either."

Dylan held out a hand and Hope handed the clue list over to him. He pocketed a hand as he looked over the last line.. *Sweet smelling and random well wishes.* "Who made these up?" he asked, handing the list back to her, and pocketing his other hand. "I have no idea either."

"Well, what are sweet smelling things? Let's start there." Hope's brow crinkled as she thought.

"Sweet smelling could be anything," Dylan said, "Food, flowers, perfume—"

"Flowers? It could be flowers." Hope pushed off from the bus and started pacing. "Think, Hope, think."

"Random means unexpected, unplanned, by chance, etcetera." Dylan thought out loud.

"And well wishes …" Hope said. "That's self-explanatory."

Dylan turned to face Hope. "If we're going with flowers, then the 'sweet smelling' part could mean random gifting of flowers to someone."

"We're done. Let's go!" Katie led the youth back onto the minibus.

Hope squinted at him as she thought, and Dylan gestured for them to get back on the minibus. They were so close.

As the last of their team filed inside, Dylan closed the doors and drove the minibus out of the fuel station. Hope swiveled in her seat to discuss the next clue with their team. Sandbar Drive was quiet this time of night, and Dylan tried to piece together the clues as he drove past the row of upper-class houses decorated for Christmas. The bright seasonal lights were interrupted by the soft amber lights of the private, catching Dylan's attention. The clues fell into place in his mind, and he pulled over.

"Guys, we need to take flowers to a random patient at the hospital." He made a U-turn and turned back to the hospital.

As soon as Dylan pulled into the hospital carpark and killed the engine, Hope unclasped her seatbelt. "I've got this. I'll buy some flowers from the gift shop, it'll still be open." She jumped down from her seat and exited the minibus, followed by the rest of the youth.

Dylan waited with the bus while his team disappeared inside the hospital. Bored, he drummed his fingers on the steering wheel. How was the other team going? How was Nick doing? He pulled out his phone to message his mate, stomach bugs were never fun. Lights flashed in his peripheral and he looked up to see the other minibus entering the car park.

The lights swung out wide and pulled up across the lot from him. Moments later, a team of youth thundered past him towards the hospital with Trent in hot pursuit. Dylan smirked. Hope had a good ten minutes' lead on them. Confident in their position, he pulled out the checklist to mark off their last challenge. A knock sounded on his window, and he jumped.

He turned to find Lexi smiling up at him. Without second thought, he tossed the list aside and pulled his window open. "Hey!"

"Hey, yourself!" Her tone was light and expression teasing as she looked up at him, her hair aglow in the light of the setting sun. "What number is this stop for you?"

Dylan matched her easy grin with one of his own. "Last one for us. What about you guys?"

They hadn't been alone together since that night at Hope's place, and he wondered if that was why she chose to talk to him from outside the bus, instead of coming inside.

"Last one for us, too," Lexi said, her tone oozing confidence.

"We're going down to the wire again, like the last time our teams faced off against each other," Dylan said. "Remember how that one ended?"

"I think we'll win this time," she said with a tip of her chin before casting a glance back at the hospital.

Hope burst through the reception doors, followed by his team. He chuckled. "No chance. You have Trent on your team."

Lexi turned back to him and raised an eyebrow. "What's that supposed to mean?"

"Hey, Lexi." Hope called as she shepherded the youth onto the bus. "Trent's still chatting with the patient. See you back at the Walkers."

Dylan thumbed towards Hope as he started the bus. "That's what I mean."

Without waiting for another comment, Dylan drove the bus out of the hospital car park. He couldn't help but laugh as he spied Lexi checking her watch in the rearview mirror. "I love the man, Hope, but he can't help it. I knew we had this in the bag as soon as I saw Trent follow the youth inside."

"I know. Why would Lexi send him into a hospital?"

Dylan smiled and glanced at Hope. "He would have volunteered."

# SIX

The minibus tires crunched to a halt on the stone driveway at the Walkers, and Dylan killed the engine. Hope was out of her seat and shepherding the youth off the bus before Dylan had a chance to say, "C'mon guys, let's finish this!"

The deep indigo evening sky was fading into pastel pink and orange that lined the horizon as Dylan rounded the Walker's homestead and caught up with his team huddle on the lawn. Cory was reading out the last clue of their Random Acts of Kindness car rally. His hands shook with excitement and he pranced on the spot. There was a distinct rumble in the distance of the other minibus weaving down the long winding driveway, and Dylan cast a quick glance over his shoulder. The other team was closing in on them and would show up any minute.

"I don't know." Cory stared at the paper in his hands.

"C'mon guys, think. They're coming." Matt took the paper off Cory and looked at Hope. "Hope, what do you think?"

Dylan turned his attention back to the huddle and plucked the piece of paper out of Matt's hand. "Ok, guys. Relax. Just relax. We've had them beat at every turn so far, and we're not about to lose it now." Dylan said, voice steady despite the churning within his stomach. They were not going down tonight.

He scanned the word on the page, then read out loud to his team. "I am full, but there is always room. Laughter is shared, but also tears. Come alone, or with friends, I'm always there with something to share."

"It's the end of the challenge, so the answer has to be here." Hope said.

"I think it has to be something inside." Katie twirled her long plait between her fingers. "Because what outside is ever full?"

Dylan nodded. He looked over the expanse of land stretching out from the lights of the house out to where the darkness swallowed it up, and back to the house. Katie had a good point.

Inside? He frowned in thought.

"What about the kitchen?" Marcus pulled on Dylan's arm.

Thundering footsteps approached. The din of laughter and chatter grew louder and louder until Trent and Lexi's team burst into view. Behind him, Dylan's team grew anxious and distracted.

"Focus, team." He locked eyes with Hope.

The dining room. They mouthed to one another.

Careful not to give the clue away to the nearby team, they huddled the team in. Hope's face flushed with excitement as she hushed those near her. She got as excited as the young people on these game nights.

"Ok, team. We need to get to the dining room." Dylan whispered. "On the count of three, we race in." Holding a finger up, Dylan started the count.

1 ...

The noise from the other team grew, their shouted suggestions echoing over the night sky.

2 ...

Hooded plovers called to each other above them as Dylan's team stood poised, every muscle tensed, waiting for the final count.

3!

Like horses bolting from the starting gate, Dylan's team—including Hope—raced past him, headed for the dining room. Trent and Lexi turned to face him, and he smiled in triumph, gave a lazy salute, then turned and sprinted after his team.

\* \* \*

"How did you get through it so quick?" Lexi asked, draining her glass of lemon water and putting the empty glass on the table.

Dylan shrugged, his smile teasing. "Guess we were the superior team."

"Amen, brother!" Hope high-fived him as Lexi and Trent exchanged a sickened glance. Dylan laughed, poured himself a glass of water from one of the jugs on the table, and sat back in his chair. The Walkers had outdone themselves tonight.

Their dining room had been utterly transformed. The south-facing floor-to-ceiling, glass doors had been opened up, allowing the warm summer breeze in, along with the soothing sounds of the trees rustling in the moonlit yard. The overhead lighting had been dimmed to allow the three five-arm candelabras lining the trestle table to warmly light the room, while the gentle flicker of fairy lights behind the white draping chiffon curtains against the walls created a heavenly feel. The table was laden with platters of fruit, trays of savories, steaming soups, and jugs of lemon water.

Dylan took a sip of his drink before replacing his glass on the table and linking his hands behind his head. Gentle murmurings of conversation floated on the air around him. Tonight felt good. Car rally's, he liked. Car rallies with meaning, he loved.

Pastor Walker rose and moved to stand in the open doorway, his large frame silhouetted by the lighting illuminating the alfresco area behind him.

He delivered his message to the young people in his usual straight-talking way. Dylan found himself drawn into the message more than usual.

One thing he loved about youth night was that the talk at the end was straight to the point. Long, lingering messages lost the youth—and him. He gained much more from private reading and conversing in his small bible study group than at church. He knew he'd grown steadily in faith and knowledge over the years, but tonight's message was a question he'd never considered before. How did his everyday actions, words, and decisions impact those around him? Was he a positive witness for Jesus or a negative one? Could people see Jesus in him?

"Every day, we have the ability to make choices which lead people towards a relationship with Jesus or turn them away from Him. I challenge you all, as you leave here tonight, to seize each day and make a difference in someone's life, to reflect the character of Jesus to everyone you meet."

Dylan turned his butter knife end over end on the table as he listened. He couldn't deny the sudden bloom of eagerness swelling within him. Imagine making a difference in people's lives every day.

"Hey, D, you paying attention?" Trent asked.

Dylan glanced over his shoulder at Trent and nodded. "Yeah …Yeah, I am. Just thinking."

"What's on your mind?"

He smiled at Trent. "Thinking how great it would be to really share our faith every day, to be the witness the Bible calls us to be."

"I find it hard to witness at the store." Hope rested her chin in her hands. "I mean, how does that go? 'That'll be $5.95 and do you know Jesus?'"

Trent chuckled. "It'd show more in the way you serve people. Let your smile be genuine. Let your service to each customer be above and beyond. Let your conversation hold no gossip but be uplifting at all times."

Dylan looked over at Lexi. Her face was illuminated in a smile and he couldn't help but smile himself. "What are you thinking, Lex?"

Her eyes flicked to his. "I'm thinking I know who we can invite to come to Youth Night in the New Year. Have any of you heard of the Christian youth organization 'His Hands?'"

Dylan shook his head and looked at his friends, their expressions were blank as well. He turned back to Lexi. This sounded interesting.

"They perform local mission work across the state. Soup kitchens, food drives, fundraisers, building projects, garage sales, and loads more. I reckon we get them to come speak at youth one night and offer our young people the opportunity to put their faith into action. You know, help them understand how to be a witness."

"That sounds amazing." Hope said. "I certainly can use a few tips."

"Well, tonight impacted me." Dylan sat back in his chair. "The message makes me want to change a few things in my life so I can help people more."

Dylan's phone rang. He pulled it from his back pocket to check who the caller was. Coach Davis. Why was he calling him on a Friday night? Curious, Dylan excused himself from the table and slipped from the dining room and out into the wide timber-lined hallway. Once the door had closed behind him, he swiped his finger across the screen to answer the call. He didn't even get the chance to speak a greeting before his coach's booming voice came down the line.

"Dylan. I just had a call from the Condor's Football Club. They want you!"

# SEVEN

The weekend was dragging.

Thoughts of a career with the Australian Football League both thrilled and humbled Dylan, and he couldn't keep a thought in his mind. His stomach had been in knots from the moment he'd disconnected the call last night, and he knew it wouldn't ease until after the secret meeting scheduled for tomorrow morning. He'd been so distracted at church that he couldn't even recall what the sermon was about. When he arrived home, he'd walked straight past Jack wrestling with changing a flat tire on his car. The argument that followed quickly snapped him out of his daydreaming.

From his position on the front lawn, Dylan sighed heavily as he took in their quiet home. He felt caged up inside, so ambled outside to watch the sun set only to find himself surrounded by jobs that needed doing. As the sun slipped below the horizon and murky shadows lengthened along the uncut lawn, Dylan sighed again. Jack had disappeared in a huff and Mum declared she wasn't hungry then retired for the evening, so Dylan was left with a long evening ahead to amuse himself.

The meeting with his coach and club president at eight tomorrow morning wouldn't come fast enough and Dylan found himself pacing. He had to find something to do. Sleep wasn't going to be possible, so there was no point going to bed. It was growing dark outside, so he couldn't do any jobs outside. TV bored him. He didn't want to read, although he probably should. He thought about his Bible. A hare darted across the lawn and he followed the animal's furious pace until it disappeared behind the shed.

Maybe he'd take the bike out.

Maybe. He'd go visit Lexi. The idea of visiting Lexi overrode the constant thoughts about an AFL career that had been plaguing him all day and he enjoyed the reprieve. Before giving himself chance to change his mind, he headed inside to grab his keys and get going.

But he felt unsettled as he coasted through town. The turn-off to the Lexi's was coming up, a turn he'd taken many times before, but now he wasn't sure. He pressed the bike on and tried to ignore any worrying thoughts. He'd visit Lexi, just like the many other times he'd visited her in the past. Whatever would happen would happen.

The house was in darkness when he pulled the bike up, and he couldn't deny the sense of disappointment that washed over him. He looked at his watch. It was after nine, and she hadn't said if she had plans tonight—or if she had, he couldn't remember. He'd knock on the door anyway. Decided, he pulled off his helmet and headed to the front door.

His knock echoed through the house, but there was silence inside. Even though he was sure no one was home, he waited a moment longer before turning back to his bike. He'd grab some takeaways and head home. Straddling his bike, he sent a quick a message to Lexi to say he'd stopped by, then kicked the bike into life and headed back towards town.

Hook & Cook, The Valley's premier fish and chip takeaway cafe, was bustling when he pushed through the double glass doors and approached the wooden counter to place his order. While perusing the specials board, he felt a grin spread upon his face. Would a career in the AFL would cramp his taste for greasy fish and chips? Maybe, but that wasn't tonight. After placing an order for large chips—no salt—two grilled barramundi, two potato cakes, steamed dim-sims, and a corn jack, Dylan moved to the waiting area. His phone vibrated in his pocket, and his heart geared up a notch when he saw a message from Lexi.

*Hey you, sorry I'm out at grandma's 80th tonight. Catch up tomorrow?*

He wouldn't get to catch up with her tonight. Disappointing. He was about to agree with her offer to catch up tomorrow when he remembered the meeting with his club. The pangs of nerves and excitement clashed within him again. He hit reply.

*Got club business tomorrow, will let you know if we're let out early. Don't overdo the scones with jam and cream!*

"Order for Saunders."

He tucked his phone in his pocket and rose to collect his order. As he headed for the counter, his phone buzzed again. He scooped up his order, he tucked the warm bundle under his arm, and headed back to his bike, pulling the phone out as he went.

*Too late. Food coma. Need help!*

He smiled. What she said was more true than funny he thought as he tucked his food into the bike's leather saddlebag, then headed home.

\* \* \*

Dylan strode into the clubrooms with more confidence than he was feeling, letting the doors close loudly behind him. Coach Davis and Club President Michael Smith were seated at the bar. They looked up as he approached.

"Good morning, fellas."

"Dylan, welcome!" Michael rose from the bar stool he was perched on and held out a hand. "Have a seat."

Dylan grasped the hand Michael extended him and shook it firmly before taking the vacant seat and crossed his arms. The meeting was unexpected and while he'd had a day to prepare for what was about to be discussed, he still wasn't ready. But he'd done all he could do—pray.

A firm hand clamped on his shoulder and he turned to look at his coach. "Well, son, you know what this meeting is about. What's your initial feeling on the topic?"

"I'm shocked." Dylan answered seriously though his answer brought hearty chuckles from his superiors. He glanced between them, then fixed his gaze on Michael as the older man leaned forward and clasped his hands over his knees. "Dylan, it was a shock for us, too. One minute we're offing you the captaincy of our local club, next minute the big time is after you! We now know talent scouts for the Condors have been lurking for some months and they like what they see."

"We've had no idea." Coach Davis dug into the bowl of peanuts sitting on the bar counter, the salt granules sticking to his chubby fingers.

Dylan thought back over the season, trying to remember what had been so outstanding about his game that he'd drawn such attention. He ran both hands over his hair, linked his fingers behind his neck and let out a frustrated growl. "I don't know. I mean, I just accepted captaincy for the Tigers. Do I just drop you—"

"Dylan, stop." Coach Davis dusted the salt from his fingers. "We're not talking about deciding what to eat for tea or what movie to watch. This opportunity is a life changer. And these opportunities don't come knocking every day."

Michael's words held a note of smug self-assurance as he tucked his chin in, allowing a distracting triple chin to appear against the collar of his grey shirt.

Were Michael's words meant to be supportive or discouraging? Dylan cleared his throat, ignoring the thought. "When do they want an answer?"

"You let us know what you'd like to do, then we'll tee up a meeting with the club and go from there."

Dylan relaxed, encouraged by coach's ear-to-ear grin. Coach Davis had been a part of his life since he was ten and was practically a father to him. "I'd like to have a chat with my family before making any decisions. Can we catch up towards the end of the week, say Thursday?"

Michael stood and extended his hand. "That's fine, son. It's a big decision. Looking forward to hearing your answer."

Dylan shook the president's hand, then coach's, and thanked the men for their time before heading out of the clubrooms.

One week to decide the rest of his life.

Right ...

# EIGHT

"Are you serious?"

Nick's voice rang with disbelief moments before his face appeared above Dylan. "The Condors Football Club want you?"

Dylan strained beneath the 125 kilogram weight he insisted on bench pressing, took a few quick breaths, then pushed the bar up while Trent spotted. His calm countenance was a contrast to Nick's disbelieving distress.

"Don't distract him, Nick." Trent said, his steady hands following the bar.

"I'm not distracting him. He brought the topic up."

Dylan brought the weights down and let the bar rest just above his chest. The men's weights room at The Valley Gymnasium was empty at this time on a Sunday evening, which was why this was their favorite time to meet and work out together. Also, it became their debriefing time about each other work and private lives. To Dylan, gym night was his favorite night in the week after Youth night.

Dylan pushed the bar back up. "No, Nick, I'm joking. I thought it would be a fun story to make up." Nick's face showed a look of disgust, then disappeared from his vision. An exercise bike geared up moments later.

Dylan focused on finishing his reps, trying not to let his thoughts deviate onto what a career with the AFL would be like. Never in his wildest fantasy would he have thought an AFL club would be interested in him. Now one was, he doubted his ability. What did they see in him?

"Come on; that'll do. You've done ten more than your normal reps. You'll drop the bar in a minute." Trent lifted the bar out of Dylan's hands and guided it into the cradle. Breathing heavily, Dylan rested his hands limply across his chest and waited a moment before sitting up. Trent disappeared and Dylan heard the zip of weights running up and down wires. He stared at the ceiling, catching his breath.

The idea of him playing AFL sounded more and more fanciful.

Restless, he pushed himself up. Whipping his sports towel off the nearby Power Tower, he wiped the sweat off his face and around the back of his neck. "I need to give the club an answer by the end of the week and I'm completely stuffed about what to do."

"How … is this … a difficult … decision?" Nick asked in between puffs. His face reddened with effort as his powerful thighs strained against the bike.

Dylan hung his arms off the towel across the back of his neck and groaned. "I just accepted the captaincy of the Tigers. So has this opportunity just happened to pop up because I've made the wrong decision, or is this a distraction opportunity because I've made the right decision?"

"You're … thinking … too much."

Dylan looked across the room at Trent, caught his friend's steady gaze and shrugged. "What do you think?"

Trent paused in his reps and rested his arms off the lateral raise bar. Dylan knew that look. He was about to be challenged.

"No. I think serious consideration is needed in this case. One thing I will say is, you prayed specifically about something and an answer has been given to you …"

There it was. Everything was always so clear to Trent. His answers to problems were uncomplicated and straightforward. Nothing seemed to worry him. Dylan seated himself at the Pec Deck and roughly set his weights. His muscles were already straining and his muscle fibers were trembling, but he ignored them. Much like Trent's advice. He knew what Trent was driving at with his comments—he'd asked God directly if he should captain the Tigers and it'd been given to him. But, then again, it wasn't every day an AFL club wanted you.

"I know what you're saying, Trent," Nick said between puffs, slowing his cycling down. "But I still think he's overthinking. God gives us talents and requires us to not only use them but to grow them as well. What better way to grow a talent in football than to take it to the highest level?"

"Our talents are to edify and glorify God." Trent resumed his weights, grunting as he pulled the bar down. "So which option does that?"

Knowing the question was aimed at him, Dylan pulled the arms pads together forcefully and let them out slowly. He'd hoped asking the boys for their thoughts on the situation would help make things clearer, but he agreed with both of their opinions, leaving him no more enlightened.

He would discuss it with his family over dinner. Hopefully some family counsel would help him rest easier with the decision he needed to make. Either way things played out, his gut said he'd regret something. And that thought sat like a lead weight in his stomach.

# NINE

The warm scents of basil and mozzarella greeted Dylan as he climbed the front porch steps of the family home. It was a typical early summer evening in The Valley, warm and muggy, and he felt good. A hot shower after his workout had done wonders for his mood and now the looming decision mountain seemed more like a molehill.

Somewhere between leaving the gym and arriving home the uncomfortable lump of uncertainty sitting in his guts had shifted. The more he thought about it, the more he saw the opportunity placed before him as a blessing. He was sure his family would agree.

"Mum?" He called out, closing the door behind him. To his right, the air conditioner hummed and the TV flickered in the darkened lounge room. He peeked his head in. Jack was slumped in the lazyboy, facing the TV, with a hand resting on the remote, eyes unblinking.

"Is Mum home?" Dylan asked.

"Kitchen." Jack said, changing the TV channel. Police sirens and human wailing rang out from the set as Dylan left the room and crossed the hall to the kitchen.

Mum looked up from setting the table as he entered, her countenance brightening when she saw him. "Hello, sweetie. How was your day?"

"It was … good." How could he describe his day? It had been an emotional rollercoaster.

"Well, see if you can uproot your brother from that TV and get him to come in here. I'm about to dish up dinner. Then you can tell us about your day."

Ten minutes and an argument with Jack later, Dylan joined his family at the dining table. Spaghetti Bolognese. Again. Masking his disappointment, he twirled spaghetti on his fork and kicked Jack under the table as he started to complain about his meal. "Guys, there's something I wanted to talk to you about. That is, unless there is any family business we need to chat about first?"

"Nothing from me." Jack slurped spaghetti into his mouth.

"What did you want to talk to us about, sweetie?"

Dylan took a deep breath and looked from his Mum's interested expression to the disinterest on Jack's face. He'd just blurt it out. How his family reacted was in God's hands. "Well, as you know, I went to the clubhouse this morning for a meeting with Coach Davis and the club president. They wanted to tell me that an AFL club has made enquiries about me."

Jack turned to look at him and Dylan grinned slightly as he looked at Mum. She lowered her fork and raised her eyes to his.

"What are these enquires they've made?"

"Come on, Mum!" Jack said. "They don't want to know his favorite color. They obviously want him for their team next year."

"Show some respect, Jack."

"She's always asking stupid questions."

Distracted, Dylan glared at Jack while he continued to shovel spaghetti into his mouth, his fork scrapping loudly along his plate with no regard for his cutting comment. A thought flashed through Dylan's mind: if he accepted the Condors proposition, it'd require more of his time. Who'd be around to watch and guide Jack? Would Mum be ok?

Uncertainty nipped again in the corners of his mind.

"An AFL club wants you to play for them next year?" Mum asked, her voice holding a note of timidity. "Which club? You don't have to move interstate or anything, do you?"

"No. I wouldn't need to move. It's with the Melbourne Condors, and they want an answer by Friday. The contract is ready. I just have to say yes or no." Appetite waning, Dylan put his spaghetti-laden fork down and reached for the plastic jug of water to pour himself a glass.

"I think you should take it, bro. It's the big time."

"Your brother is right." Mum's voice was barely louder than a whisper. "These opportunities don't come around every day, and it would set you up for life. Do you know what the contract says?"

Dylan shook his head. "We'll go over that at our next meeting."

Mum twirled her spaghetti onto her fork and daintily took a bite, smiling at Dylan with her eyes. "Make sure you read the details. The devil is in the fine print, remember."

Dylan hummed in agreement. "I might give Uncle Shane a call and have a chat to him about it."

Mum nodded her approval and went back to her meal.

Dylan sat back in his chair, watching Mum and Jack finish their dinner in silence. Only the clatter of Jack's fork on his plate and the tick of the clock above the stove filled the air. His mind felt like a can of worms with ideas rolling and weaving over one another, so slick and fleeting that he couldn't seem to grasp them. If this was such a great opportunity, why was he feeling at odds over it? Mum was right. The devil was in the fine print, but maybe the devil was right there in front of him as well. He needed to pray about it. Guilt pricked his mind.

Prayer ... Frustrated, he finished his dinner, scooped up his plate and took it to the sink. Seeing Jack's empty plate and his attention now focused on his lap—no doubt on his phone—he scooped up his plate and took it to the sink as well.

"Leave the dishes, honey," Mum joined him at the sink. "It's Jack's turn to—"

"I'm not washing the damn dishes, so stop asking." Jack stood and left the room, his shoulders hunched forwards as he remained immersed in his phone.

Mum tugged the dishcloth from his hands, and Dylan looked at her. "It's ok, Mum. I'll wash up." Dylan reached to take back the cloth, but she didn't let go.

A muscle twitched in her jaw. He hated the way Jack treated her and did what he could to help out, but his best efforts couldn't erase the hurt Jack caused. A sheen formed over her eyes and he quietly left the room.

The evening had turned uncharacteristically cool for the time of year. Dylan pushed his bedroom window open and took a deep breath of the crisp air. Everything was silhouetted by the full moon shining like a new pearl through the pitch-colored sky, from the post-and-rail fences next door to the still forms of the neighbors' horses sleeping in their paddock. All was at peace. All except the thoughts in his mind.

He reached for his phone and dialed Uncle Shane. The line rang out, so he sent a text message asking Shane to give him a call back about a football question. That would get him ringing back quickly. Then he turned back to the view out his window and knelt.

Desperate to know he was making the right decision in God's will for his life, Dylan turned his gaze heavenward. "What do I do, Lord? Show me. Give me a sign so I know which road to take. Do I keep the captain's role at the Tigers, or do I take the AFL career?"

# TEN

"Dylan, I could use a hand over here if you're free." Matt Laker's voice boomed across the workshop floor.

"Be with you in a sec, boss," Dylan called back.

The impact gun felt good in his hands, and the prime mover's lug nuts were coming free easily. Thankfully. The truck's suspension needed a lot of work and the bearings needed to be replaced before the driver came back this afternoon, but time was against him. As the vibrations ran up his arms and through his chest, filling the workshop with the sharp machine-gun like rattle, Dylan tried not to think of the ever-growing list of jobs on his run sheet. As soon as the wheel was off, Dylan yanked the earmuffs from his head and crossed the floor towards the grease pit where his boss was working.

"What's up boss?" Dylan asked, hunkering down.

"I need to completely overhaul this trucks air brake system." Matt said. "Can you clear my schedule? I'm going to be here all day."

Clear the schedule. Sure. Where would he clear Matt's jobs to? "There's already a backlog. Do you want me to stay back tonight?"

Matt cursed and Dylan held back a chuckle as his boss wiped brake fluid from his face. "No, you can head off at your normal time. Just get that schedule cleared off for me as soon as you can."

"Excuse me, fellas?" A male voice echoed across the workshop floor.

Dylan stood and turned to face the approaching customer. The man looked to be in his mid-forties, with weather-beaten features from years working in the sun, and an extended hand the size of baseball mitt. Large and rough and calloused. Dylan clasped it firmly. "How can I help you, sir?"

"My word lad, you're built like a brick outhouse! What are you, six foot four?"

"Six-five." Dylan was proud of his height and liked the fact he was solid as well. Coach Davis often commented that while he'd most likely stopped growing height-wise, he would continue filling out for a few more years to come. "How can I help you?"

"Got a grip like a vice as well." The man took off his cap, scratched his head and slapped the cap back on. "Do you know anything about bobcats?" Dylan nodded, ignoring the comment about his handshake. He was all too aware of the mountain of work waiting for him, so he had to keep the man on topic. "Of course. What's the problem?"

"Seems the ol' lift and tilt components are playing up. When could you look at it?"

Dylan crossed his arms while he thought. He couldn't commit to anything until he'd rearranged the schedule. "At a stretch, Wednesday morning."

"Wednesday sounds great. The name's Rodger. Rodger White." Rodger reached up to slap Dylan on the shoulder. "Of White's Landscaping. I'll call you on Wednesday."

Rodger turned and headed towards the workshop entrance, Dylan turned to head to the office to begin rescheduling Matt's run sheet when Rodger called out to him. "Was there something else you wanted to discuss?" Dylan asked.

"No lad, no." Rodger crossed his arms across his sizable paunch and seemed to be sizing Dylan up.

"No, I'm curious. Do you play a sport, son?"

Dylan dipped his head and pocketed his hands. "Yeah, I play football for my local club. Why?"

"I know a few talent scouts in the AFL and I can tell you, players of your size and build are in high demand. Have you been approached?"

Last night's prayer flashed back into Dylan's mind. He blinked, surprised this conversation was taking place and here of all places, but for some unknown reason, he didn't want to reveal that he had, in fact, been made an offer. "I'm happy playing for my club, sir. But thank you for the compliment."

"Think about it." Rodger said, then handed him one of his cards. "See you Wednesday."

As Rodger disappeared from sight and Matt called him back to work, Dylan entered the workshop office and sat heavily in the boss's chair. A load rescheduling lay before him, but he couldn't help but be stirred by the conversation with Rodger. Was it a coincidence? Mum always said coincidences were just occasions where God chose to remain anonymous. Had his prayers been answered? Was God using this random yet on-topic conversation to show him the path to take? He rubbed his brow. He didn't have time to think about this right now. With a deep breath, Dylan turned the run sheet towards him and picked up the phone.

\* \* \*

The pew under Dave's library window was welcoming after Dylan's long day, and he sighed. Reorganizing Matt's work took longer than expected, and Dylan had almost cancelled coming to the leadership team meeting to prepare for youth group on Friday night. But it wouldn't be Monday without finishing the day at Dave's.

Something pressed against his lower back, and he leaned forward to pull one of the many pillows out from behind him, then relaxed again as the door opened and Nick and Hope entered. "Hope. You're usually last to arrive." Dylan said through a yawn.

"I picked her up." Nick flicked the pillows onto the chair next to him, then took a seat next to Dylan.

Hope sat down opposite them, giving Nick lengthy scowl that he seemed to miss—or ignore. Dylan chuckled to himself. Everyone knew Hope struggled to be on time, though she protested the fact every time it came up.

"Dave's on the phone," Dylan said, breaking the tension between his friends. "Not sure where Trent or Lexi are."

"Lexi's on her way. She got held up at the café," Hope said, sifting through her church bag. Dave's voice sounded beyond the library doors as he wrapped up the call. Dylan checked his watch. Ten past seven. Where was Trent? Nick checked a message he'd received on his phone.

"Ok youth leaders, let's get this meeting started," Dave said as he entered the room with a clap of his hands. "Where are Lexi and Trent?"

"On their way." Nick pocketed his phone.

As Dave settled himself behind his large mahogany desk and organized his papers, Dylan pulled out his phone and opened the memo app ready to take notes. Dave was midway through explaining the theme for the week's youth night when the library door creaked open, and Lexi slipped in. Dylan smiled at her as she slipped into the seat next to Hope, apologizing for being held up. Dave acknowledged her without pausing.

In Dylan's view, the game Dave proposed for the youth was questionable. His brow furrowed as he took notes. At one point, after exchanging a glance with Nick and seeing a sketch Nick had made, Dylan turned away stifling the urge to laugh by clearing his throat.

"Boys," Dave said. "You have questions?"

Dylan chuckled and immediately regretted it. This wasn't high school. "Sorry, Dave, no questions. Nick sketched something that distracted me." A sharp elbow nudged his ribs, and Dylan turned the threatening smile on his face downwards.

"Dave, I'm sorry, but asking the youth to perform surgery on a banana …" Nick leaned forward.

Dylan laughed then at the tone in Nick's voice, and looked up. Lexi and Hope both looked confused. He cleared his throat again as he regained his composure. "Sorry, guys. I've had a long day and I think my brain has shut down. I need a run or something." Dylan said.

The library door opened. Trent entered, his usual clean-cut appearance marred by an uncharacteristic rumpled shirt and five o'clock shadow.

"Hi guys, sorry I'm late." He hurriedly took a seat and pulled out a notepad.

Dave reshuffled his papers, then passed hand-outs to Lexi over the desk as Hope explained the plan to Trent, who looked equally doubtful at the idea of the banana game. They were going to need a debrief session at The Valley Beachside after this meeting.

# ELEVEN

The sailboat-patterned glass door swung open with a creak, and Dylan held it open for his friends as they stepped inside the Beachside hotel. There was a low din from the scattered patrons, and he breathed deeply while he followed his friends towards their preferred booth. He loved the ambiance of this hotel. It had a warmth about it, with the quiet murmurings of conversations floating on the air, the teasing scents coming from the kitchen, the clack of pool balls from the bar, and the crackle of the open fireplace in the lounge. It was one of his favorite places. That, and riding his motorbike.

"What were you boys giggling about tonight?" Hope asked as she slid into their booth.

Nick scoffed. "Didn't you hear what Dave wants us to do on Friday night?"

"It will be what we make it," Lexi said, signaling for Nick to move over on the seat so she could sit. "Besides, I think it has a good point to it and our role is to try and teach the young people, not entertain them."

Dylan shuffled down the opposite bench next to Trent and felt a pang of remorse at Lexi's words. He shouldn't have scoffed. Dave always had great ideas, but this one missed the mark. "I'm sorry, Lex, but I struggle to see how young people are going to overlook the joke and see the message."

"How are you not getting it?" Hope put the menu down with a sigh. "We give them each a banana and tell them to cut it up in as many different ways they can think of, then they have to try and put it back together –"

"Yeah but—" Nick held up a hand.

"I'm not finished, Nick," Hope said. "The banana symbolizes relationships, and chopping it up symbolizes our rash decisions within that relationship. The point is that no matter how hard they try to put the banana back together again, it will never be the same. I don't see how this is such a hard concept for you boys to get."

Nick signaled the waiter over and shrugged. "I do get it Hope, but why a banana?"

Dylan buried his face in the menu to hide his smile.

"And what is so funny about that?" Hope snipped.

Knowing the question was directed at him, Dylan glanced over the top of the laminated drinks page before him and met Hope's stern expression. He rubbed his jaw. "Let's just say, I know what Nick is saying. There are some young boys in the group who could use the opportunity to make jokes."

"Sounds like those boys are right here at this table." Hope huffed as the waiter appeared. The young man looked awkwardly at Hope before glancing around the table, his pen poised over his notepad. "Would anyone like to order?"

"We can change the object, but the lesson should remain," Lexi said before turning the waiter. "A tall iced tea, please."

"Water for me," Dylan said.

Hope flipped her bob and flashed a smile at the waiter in a sudden mood shift. "Hot chocolate, thanks."

Trent straightened in the seat beside him and shook his head. Dylan glanced at him as Nick ordered a Coke. "What's up with you tonight, brother?"

Trent sighed heavily and reached for one of the coasters piled neatly in the middle of the table. He toyed with the cardboard square advertising a local business, spinning the card on its corner. "Just I've heard some ... old acquaintances ... are back in town and I'd rather not see them."

The waiter returned and distributed their drinks.

"You, not wanting to see someone?" Hope stole a sip of Nick's Coke. "What's with that?"

Her statement vocalized everyone's thoughts, and all eyes settled on Trent. Out of all of them, he seemed to have everything most together. His peaceful character and the pearls of wisdom he often imparted had earned him the nickname 'Old Man'. To see him disheveled and clearly bothered by something was unnerving. He tossed the coaster away and looked brightly at them all.

"Let's talk about something else? Dylan, have you made a decision yet?"

"What decision?" Lexi asked, her drink poised near her mouth as she prepared to take a sip.

Lexi's question caught Dylan off guard, and he glanced at her. Questions flickered behind her eyes and color heightened in her cheeks. Everything had happened so fast, he'd not had time to tell the girls, and Trent had just dropped him in the middle of it. "I had a meeting with my coach and club president yesterday and was told the Condors have enquired about me."

"The AFL club?" Hope asked.

Dylan grinned, taking in her open-mouthed expression. "Yes, Hope, the AFL club."

"Have you made a decision?" Nick asked.

Hope's hand fell across his arm, her eyes wide and eager. "The … Condors?"

A burst of energy surged within him as he took in the expressions of expectancy on his friend's faces, while Hope's grip intensified on his arm. Mum was right. This was an opportunity of a lifetime, and it seemed God had blessed him greatly by offering this to him.

"I'm close to deciding." Dylan toyed with his glass of water. "I want to talk to my uncle first, but I'm thinking I'll take it."

Hope squealed and Nick slouched back in his chair, away from her. Dylan laughed as she clapped happily, drawing the attention of the nearby tables. But Lexi looked embarrassed at the attention, and swatted at Hope, hushing her. Hope quickly countered by swatting Lexi back. Her laughter floated over the room and Nick leaned forward, putting himself out of the way of the play fight. His grey eyes fixed on Dylan with tried patience as he was jostled by the girls.

"She'll be unbearable if you take this. You know that, right?"

A knowing smiled crept upon Dylan's face as he considered Nick's assessment of Hope. He was right.

But it wasn't her attention he was interested in.

# TWELVE

"Dylan, welcome."

Dylan cleared his throat and grasped the cool hand of Lachlan Ward, President of the Condor Football Club. "Thank you for the chance to meet with you, sir. It's an honor."

Lachlan gestured to the leather tub chairs overlooking the Condor's home ground and waited for Dylan to sit before he did likewise. "I understand your current coach and club president will be joining us shortly. Until they arrive, I wonder if we might get to know each other a little."

The man was physically imposing, even to Dylan. Everything he wore, from his tailored charcoal suit, black shirt, and baby pink tie down to his highly polished black shoes revealed his confidence. His dark brown eyes were shrewd and intelligent, and the no-nonsense set of his jaw suggested he wasn't a man to waste time. He was grateful for the conversation he'd had with Uncle Shane about clubs and contracts. While his uncle never played professional football, he had been approached and had discussions with an AFL club, but turned the opportunity down. It was handy to have an inside glimpse at the difference between local footy and professional footy and what would be required of him.

Lachlan crossed his legs and steepled his fingers, eyeing Dylan with a penetrating gaze. "We have been watching you this last year, Dylan, and are very keen to have you join the Condors Football Club. Have you come to us with good news?

"Mr. Ward—"

"Lachlan, please."

"Sorry, Lachlan." Dylan said, "I have given your request much thought, and it would be my pleasure to wear the black and orange guernsey next year."

Lachlan clapped once as he sat forward. "Dylan, that is brilliant news."

The large oak door to the member's room opened behind him. Dylan turned to see three men he recognized join them. Lachlan stood to face the guests, and Dylan followed suit.

"Dylan, let me introduce you to the captain of the Condors, Daniel Marshall." Lachlan indicated the man on the left, then the other two. "Our courageous full forward, Adam Cox, and our ruckman—your study—Jason Walsh."

Dylan shook each of their hands, scarcely believing this wasn't a dream.

Daniel Marshall was an imposing man in person, although a little shorter than Dylan at six foot four inches, with a thick head of brown hair and a thick well-manicured beard. Dylan knew from watching him play on TV that the man commanded a presence on the field, but the way he filled a room by just being in it was something else. His dark, piercing eyes reminded Dylan of a bird, ironically, and he found himself feeling a little intimated.

"Terrific to finally meet you," Daniel said, laying a firm hand on his shoulder. "Welcome to the Condors."

"Will you be joining us for summer training camp?" Adam asked.

Adam, the shortest man of the three, had a cultured accent and the appearance of a banker, not at all what Dylan would have imagined. He'd seen Adam play. The man was fierce on field.

"He'd better be. I've got a lot to teach the boy," Jason said as he laid a tattooed arm over Dylan's shoulders. Dylan grinned and turned to look at Jason at eye level. The young man's sandy blond hair, worn back in a small ponytail on game days, sat scruffily upon his head. "I'm going to be your shadow, mate," Dylan said.

With an easy laugh, Dylan and Lachlan resumed their seats as Daniel, Adam, and Jason joined them. The conversation flowed and Dylan listened and joined in occasionally, overwhelmed by the sense of belonging he felt. These were the men he'd watched every weekend on TV. He'd taken notes on how they played and listened with interest when they were interviewed on football shows. These guys were now his teammates. God was good!

The oak doors opened and closed again, and Dylan heard the voices of his old Tigers coach and old Tigers club president. He turned in his seat as they approached, smiling broadly at their friendly faces.

"Have we missed the contract signing?" Michael extended a hand to Lachlan. Lachlan stood and shook Michael and Coach

Davis's hands, then smiled at him. Dylan waited, unsure what was to happen next.

"Not yet, gentlemen," Lachlan answered, "Dylan, how about we get this paperwork out of the way so we can sit down and have lunch together?"

Dylan rose as Jason slapped him on the back. "Good on you, mate. See you when you get back."

With a quick dip of his head to acknowledge Jason's comment, Dylan followed Lachlan from the room, his heart beating faster than he could count.

\* \* \*

The house was quiet when Dylan arrived home. Good.

Looking down at the slick black with orange piping sports bag in his hand, he swallowed. Time felt like it had stopped today. With a pen stroke, he'd signed a contract he had never dreamed of signing and taken a defining step towards a career he had never dreamed of having. While it meant saying goodbye to Matt at the garage, he could always come back to a career as a diesel mechanic after he hung up the football boots. He'd give Matt notice Monday morning at work.

He blew his breath out, sat the bag on the kitchen table and unzipped it. Reverently, he pulled out his new guernsey and stared at the silken black with a bright orange condor in full flight logo. He'd wear this each week from now until he retired. He turned it over and ran a hand over the white numbers on the back. His new number: twenty-seven. A flicker of guilt played on his mind at leaving behind his old number ten. Ten had been on his guernseys since he was eight years old, when his dad enrolled him in Aus Kick. A lump formed in his throat at the thought of his dad.

He wished he could tell him of this moment. His hand curled around the dog tag his dad had given him: 'Paid in Full' inscribed on one side, 'Joshua 1:9' inscribed on the other.

After a moment, Dylan cleared his throat and flicked the new guernsey over his shoulder along with the memories. Dad would be proud. He would have encouraged this step. A deep breath filled his lungs as Dylan continued going through his new sports bag. Everything smelled new and felt … expensive. A grin tugged on the corner of his mouth as he remembered the details of his contract.

He was set up for life. Just like Mum had said.

He snagged his new water bottle from the bag, crossed the room to the sink, and filled it with water. While the bottle filled, Dylan looked out the kitchen window. Everything looked the same. The uncut law, the weeds growing over the chicken wire fence, the neighbor's run-down shed with the fallen-in roof and that old yellow dog on its chain, sleeping peacefully in the sun. All the same as every other time he'd looked out this window. But somehow, everything felt different.

Adrenaline pumped.

He needed to run.

# THIRTEEN

ylan returned from his run, jogged up the porch steps, and into the house. The lights were off and the TV silent as he slowed his pace to a fast stride towards the bathroom. It was odd for both Mum and his brother to be out at this time of the evening, but he didn't have time to worry about their whereabouts right now. Youth started in under an hour, along with the dreaded banana game. Just the memory made him laugh as he stepped into the shower. He and Nick had a bet as to how long it would be until the first kid laughed, and Dylan was sure he had it in the bag.

Ten minutes later and fresh from the shower, Dylan was pulling on his favorite pair of distressed jeans and surf branded T-shirt when he heard his mobile ringing on the kitchen counter. As he hurried from his room, he scooped up his wallet and keys off the dresser and pulled his bedroom door shut before jogging down the hall to the kitchen.

"Dylan speaking."

"Dylan." Adam's friendly voice greeted him. "What are you up to tonight?"

"Tonight?" Dylan asked, casting a glance at the kitchen clock. He was due at church in fifteen minutes. Should he tell Adam about his involvement in Friday night youth group? "What's on tonight?"

"A few of the boys are coming 'round to my place tonight for a few drinks and shoot some pool. Thought I'd give you a call and ask if you'd like to join us. What do you say? Are you busy?"

A perfect opportunity to meet his new teammates and start building the important relationships that would bind them together on the field lay before him, and he was hesitating. Why? The answer should come easy. Frustrated, he ran a hand over his hair. "Yeah, I kinda am busy. Sorry, Adam. I'd have loved to come."

"It's ok, mate." Adam said. His voice held a light tone which eased the tightness in Dylan's chest. "It's short notice, I understand. Heads up though: we generally get together on a Friday night—that is, if we're not out on the field, or traveling interstate. We just rotate around the boy's houses. It's good bonding time."

The tightness resumed in Dylan's chest. "Every Friday night?"

"Yeah. We're a pretty social club." Adam said.

"Everyone goes?" Dylan asked, already dreaded the answer.

"Within reason. Not everyone is free every week. Some of the fellas like to spend time with their families or girlfriends. You know because, between the training, the workouts, workshops, games, social requirements, media detail, and recovery sessions, they don't get much of a look-in sometimes." Adam finished with a laugh.

Dylan chuckled along with him. While he sounded the part, something inside him dulled a little. He knew things were going to get busy, but Adam's words seemed to bring it crashing down on him. Dylan looked at the clock again. "Sounds great, but I'm just about to head out the door. Can I take a rain check?"

"Sure thing, no worries." Adam said. "Catch up with you next week."

"See you then, Adam."

Dylan ended the call and leaned against the kitchen bench. The soothing silence of the house now felt oppressive. He rubbed his forehead wearily. How was he going to continue his commitments to youth group if there were club functions every Friday?

It would be expected that he be there. Part of team building …

He sighed. Life was about to get uncomfortably busy. And awkward.

His phone beeped with a message and he turned it towards him. Lexi. He snatched the phone up and opened his messages.

*'You coming tonight? I've got a banana here with your name all over it!'*

\* \* \*

By the time he pulled up in the church car park, Dylan was late. He hated being late, particularly for youth events. It sent the wrong message to the young people. With a quick flick of the chin strap, he removed his helmet and locked up the bike before jogging around the building towards the kitchen door at the rear. Hopefully, the door was unlocked. He grasped the handle and breathed a sigh of relief as the door gave easily, admitting him to the darkened kitchen. After turning the lights on and checking the urn was filled, he shrugged off his bike jacket and slipped out into the hall, praying nobody would notice.

Dave had the young people's attention focused towards the stage while he explained the banana game, and Dylan crept quietly along the back wall to where his friends were gathered.

"So who cracked the first joke?" he asked, coming alongside Nick.

Without so much as a glance, Nick held up a five-dollar note. Dylan plucked the cash from his mate's hand and pocked it, restraining a chuckle.

"When did you sneak in?" Lexi asked from around Nick.

"He just arrived," Nick said.

"Sorry I'm a bit late guys, but I have some big news—"

"Shh, I think we're up." Hope tapped him on the shoulder. Turning his attention back to the stage, he watched as Dave broke the gathered youth into five small groups, then signaled for Dylan and his friends to come forward and stand at a certain spot. Once they were in position, Dave addressed the young people gathered in their groups.

"Ok, guys, you know the drill. Our leaders are going to watch each of you as you work together to dissect then reconstruct your project. Points are given for quickest time, the most secure reconstruction, and for teamwork. Remember, no less than six segmentations are to be made on your task. Go!"

Dylan clasped his hands behind his back and watched as the young people go to work. He noticed Dave avoided using the word 'banana' and wondered what shenanigans he'd missed by arriving late. He smirked. He couldn't help it. But he reined in his mirth and turned his focus onto the team in front of him to monitor their progress. As he watched, the unmistakable purpose behind the game began to resonate within him. A number of decisions had headed his way of late and he wasn't sure how to handle them. As the youth in front of him cut up and disfigured their banana then tried to put it back together again, Dylan found himself frowning in thought. However he handled what was coming would not only affect his life but the lives of those around him.

"Time!" Dave shouted from his position at the front of the hall.

Dylan jumped at Dave's sudden shout, but regained his composure quickly and pushed the disturbing thoughts from his mind. He'd just accepted a career with an AFL club. Everything would be fine. It was in God's hands, after all. He was secure in God's will for his life. Nothing was going to go wrong.

As his friends moved off the stage to fill out their team cards sharing what they had observed, the top of Dylan's team's reconstructed banana slipped off and splatted on the hall floor. The teens giggled. It was clear they weren't going to win 'best reconstruction'.

After the cards were filled in and handed back to Dave, Dylan moved to the back of the room with Trent and Hope as Lexi and Nick speared off to the kitchen for youth café duty.

"What's your big news?" Trent asked quietly.

Dylan angled his head towards Trent as they walked. "I signed a contract earlier today."

"Condors?"

"Three years, renegotiated after twelve months."

Dylan turned to Trent, grinning as he took a seat at the cafe. "Impressed?"

"What are we impressed by?" Hope asked as she pulled a chair up, then gasped in realization. "Did you take the Condors offer to join their team next year?"

"I'll tell you if you promise not to jump up and down and draw attention to us," Dylan said. Hope slumped back in her chair, and Dylan chuckled.

"Yes. I have accepted it." The burgeoning smile that took over her face spoke volumes and drove home all the more the impact his decision was going to have in all his relationships. NO. He could make this work. Nothing would change, except his job.

"Well done, brother," Trent said, offering his hand.

Dylan shook Trent's hand firmly before sitting back in his chair to listen as Dave wrapped up the evening. Dreams and fantasies pulled at his attention, drawing him to think about what it would be like to run out on the field next year with his new club. Mentally, he counted down the months until the season started next year: February was pre-season, and the Premiership Cup started in March. Three months until first bounce. It seemed too far away, and his stomach twisted in anticipation. He could almost feel the hallowed turf under his feet and feel the soft—

"Hey D, you with us, bro?"

"Sorry, what was that? Dylan asked as he sat up in his seat and turned to Trent, embarrassed to be caught daydreaming when he should be paying attention.

"The end-of-year Christmas breakup at Amaze Fun Park Dave just mentioned. Are you free, or have the Condors got your calendar filling up already?"

"When is it again?" Dylan asked.

"Sunday week." Trent said, as he rose from his seat and shouldered his bag. "Same weekend as the lighting of the Christmas Tree in Main Street."

"Yeah, I'll be there. Wouldn't miss it."

# FOURTEEN

"I knew this chat was coming," Matt said as he linked his fingers over his chest and leaned back in his office chair. The garage was quiet for a Monday morning, so Dylan had taken the opportunity to break the news to his boss over morning tea. A yawn threatened, and Dylan quickly coughed into his fist. He'd not been able to sleep much since signing the Condors contract, not to mention wondering what he'd say to his boss. Matt had looked after him throughout his apprenticeship and helped him study to pass exams. This was like a breakup he didn't want. He pulled a chair up. "Why? What do you think I'm here to talk about?"

Matt took a long slurp out of his large coffee mug and raised an eyebrow at Dylan. He was drawing this out. Dylan smirked as he relaxed back into the chair.

"How many Monday mornings have we spent jabbering about the weekend football? The games played, the late-night football shows, particularly—why I need to remind you of this, I don't know—but the player swaps, draft picks, retirements, and contract talk at the end of the year?" Matt lent forward in his chair and used his mug to emphasize his point. "I couldn't be prouder of you. First game, I want a picture blown up, framed, and signed to hang in the garage. Oh, maybe with an inscription. 'Thanks for teaching me everything I know'."

Dylan laughed. A wonderful feeling of relief coursed through him. "Everything I know? That's a big call." Matt shrugged and took a mouthful from his coffee mug again.

"You knew I was going to resign?" Dylan said, keeping his tone matter-of-fact, and helping himself to a piece of caramel slice from the morning tea plate.

Matt nodded. "Of course. No way you could perform professional football duties and continue to work at the garage. What will you do about the leadership program on Friday nights?"

Dylan cringed. "That will be tricky," he said around a mouthful of slice. "I'll hold onto it as long as I can."

A dull buzzer sounded in the garage indicating someone had pulled up. Matt craned his neck out the office window, then dusted off his hands. "Well, we both know this came up on you unexpectedly. I'm sure they'll understand over at your church."

Dylan chugged down the rest of his hot chocolate and rose to greet the visitor. "I'm sure they will. They're great."

"How much notice are you going to give me?" Matt asked as Dylan turned to leave the office.

"I'll see out the year for you."

Matt held out his hand after a moment of thought. "Four weeks is great. Thank you. Now, let's go serve this customer."

The day went by fast. The number of customers picked up and Dylan worked easily alongside Matt, relieved the conversation about his resignation was over. He knew he had to let some things go in order to move forward with his football career, he hated leaving people behind.

"Right, that's a day!" Matt called out, sliding the garage door down and clicking the latch. Dylan took a deep breath and blew it out with a huge smile. He was exhausted and looking forward to a good night sleep. After packing his tools away and collecting his gear from the tearoom, Dylan called out to Matt he was going and exited the side door. As he swung his bike jacket on, he felt his mobile vibrate in his back pocket. He zipped up his jacket and pulled out the phone to check the message.

*Last leadership team meeting for the year. Come with Christmas cheer. See you at 7.30pm. Dave.*

* * *

As expected, Dave's house looked like Christmas itself. Icicle lights hung from the guttering, and solar lit candy canes lined the walk way up to the front door. Red and green tinsel, coloured flashing lights and ornaments hung in a haphazard manner from every tree in the front yard, and Dylan could just imagine the kids had something to do with that.

Dylan pulled his bike up alongside Lexi's jeep and Trent's ute and took a moment to appreciate Dave's decorating efforts. He couldn't help but feel something special was is the air. He loved Christmas time. A blubbering, spluttering sound broke into the quiet of the evening and Dylan looked over his shoulder with a grin. Hope's car needed work again, and by the sound of it, needed it soon. Hope pulled up beside him, killed the engine, and rustled around in her handbag doing who knew what. Eventually, the door groaned open.

"Hey! What a gorgeous night! Good to see I won't be the last one to arrive this week." Hope greeted him with the exuberance of a kid about to devour a birthday cake.

"Evening, Hope." Dylan said with a chuckle. "Sounds like she's running a bit rich there ..." A frown flickered across her brow. Dylan gestured to the car. "Need me to take a look at it for you?"

Hope gave an airy wave of her hand. "Pfft, nah. Dad said he'd look at it—he says he'll be home this weekend. But thank you."

The library door stood open and Christmas music mingled with the hum of happy conversation could be heard. Dylan and Hope made their way through the house. At the last moment, Hope ducked through the doorway into the library and grandly announced she wasn't the last to arrive. Dylan rolled his eyes as he entered the room and greeted the team before taking a seat.

Everyone had their bit of Christmas cheer going on. Nick had some sort of comedic T-shirt on, Trent had a nativity belt buckle, Hope wore a pair of flashing Christmas tree earrings, and Lexi pulled out a Santa hat. Dylan couldn't help the smile that crossed his face as he looked at Lexi across the room. She looked cute. She looked at him and a blush filled her cheeks as her eyes dropped to his chest to read the message on his T-shirt. *Mistletoe. Hey, I don't make the rules.* The flicker of a smile playing upon her mouth was encouraging. He knew the inscription on his T-shirt, and he waited for her eyes to come back to his, when an elbow in his ribs drew his attention to Nick beside him.

"Did we get our shirts from the same shop?"

Dylan sat back and read Nick's. *Who needs mistletoe with a face like this?* "Nice." He laughed.

Nick flashed a cheeky grin. "Yours is pretty good too."

Hope stood and approached them, eyeing their T-shirts. "Well, Miss Fashion, whose T-shirt is the most Christmasy?" Nick asked. Hope hung her hands off her hips and hummed.

"I like both. Nick, the comment on yours is spot on—the sarcasm suits you. And Dylan, the word 'mistletoe' in big letters draws your attention, but the by-line fits you, too. It's suggestive … but kinda like a summons, isn't it?

Hope winked, then turned to take her seat, and Dylan felt the corner of his mouth tip. One thing about Hope, she always called it.

"Although I do have to wonder why you both picked mistletoe T-shirts …" Hope added as she picked up her notepad. Trent and Lexi chuckled across the room, and Dylan felt the heat lick up his neck. He shot Hope a playful scowl. He couldn't speak for Nick, but he knew why he picked this T-shirt. By the look on Lexi's face, the message had been received.

"Welcome, everyone!" Dave perched on the edge of his office desk. "We've made it to the end of our first year together, and I have to say it's been a tremendous blessing to work with each of you. But the question needs to be asked: who's going around again next year?"

Dylan looked around the room. All the hands were raised, including his own. Dave looked at him. "Dylan, you've had a massive end to the year and looks like next year will be full-on for you. Are you sure you'll have time?"

"I'd like to try. I'll know more when the schedule is handed out next year."

"I'm definitely in for next year." Hope sat forward on her seat, drummed her fingers on her notepad, and flashed a smile around the room.

Lexi nodded. "Me, too."

Dave looked to be making ticks on a run sheet. He looked up and over at Nick. "How is the city precinct working out for you?"

Nick cleared his throat. "I'm enjoying the city work, thanks. Count me in for next year."

Trent clapped Nick on the shoulder. "That's good to hear. We've been praying for you. I'm in too, Dave. Will be an honor to serve the youth again through the leadership team."

"Great." Dave said. "I'm excited about you all coming on board again. Got some new ideas I'm looking forward to sharing with the youth. Until then, it's just the final youth group of the year this Friday, and then the end-of-year breakup on Sunday. We all in?"

The room buzzed with murmurs of attendance. Dylan sat forward. "I'll be there on Sunday, but I need to put in an apology for Friday."

"Right-o, noted. Now, let's get down to business. Friday night first, then Sunday." Dave said as he moved to sit behind his desk.

The night was calm and balmy as Dylan stepped out of Dave's home with his friends an hour later. He breathed deeply of the sweet notes in the evening air while a barn owl rasped somewhere above. The night had wrapped up well. His teammates chatted about the upcoming youth night as they meandered towards their vehicles, and Dylan felt amiss knowing he wouldn't be there. He relaxed against his bike and listened to the closing conversations.

Lexi, who was just in front of him, relaxing against her car while she conversed, held his attention. If Hope and the boys left, would she linger behind?

Lexi's eyes flicked over to him and held his gaze, as if sensing his thoughts. Dylan's heart jolted. Maybe she would. The conversation around him turned into muffled background noise as his mind turned to possibilities. The air began to feel charged, and he flicked a glance at their friends, who were still engaged in conversation. Had they even noticed Lexi and himself had dropped out? He looked back at Lexi. A moment later she let her gaze drop from his, a coy grin upon her face. He wanted to push himself off the bike and step closer to her, but now was not the time.

Lexi cleared her throat as she pulled her keys out of the bag slung over her shoulder. "I better get going, guys. It's getting late." Her words were rushed and breathy and when her eyes flicked back to his, Dylan felt his pulse skyrocket. Was that an invitation to follow?

"See you Sunday?" she asked.

Nope.

Dylan dipped his head, his gaze intent. "See you then, Lex."

# FIFTEEN

With careful steps, Dylan walked his bike backwards out of the shed. Jason was hosting this week's Friday night gathering, and he didn't want to miss it. As he reached the doors, his mirrors showed Mum retuning home with something hanging out the car windows. But what? He hastened the bike backwards so he could turn around and face her.

"Hey, sweetie! Come see what I got!" She called out the car window.

He turned the bike towards the house as Mum parked the car and jump out. She raced around to the boot, flung it open, and began unloading bags of what looked like stones. After kicking out the foot stand, Dylan jogged over to her and lifted the bags out of her arms.

"What's all this?" He asked. There were more bags of stone in the boot, and two trees poked out the front passenger side window.

"Are you heading out?" Mum asked, seemingly missing his question as she lifted a large box from the boot.

"Ah, yeah, I am … I usually do on a Friday evening." Dylan stacked the bags against the steps as Mum placed the large box on the verandah. "Have you bought a pond pump? Why? We don't have a—"

"Yet!" Mum spun around from the verandah and moved to the front of the car, a noticeable skip in her step.

"What do you mean, yet? Are you going to build a pond?" Dylan asked, unable to keep the incredulous tone from his voice.

She straightened up from the car, holding a tree in each hand, appearing thoughtful. "Well, I was hoping we could build a pond."

Dylan plunged his hands into his pockets and glanced back at his bike. "Now?"

"Yes. Why not? Still plenty of light in the day."

Dylan thumbed a gesture behind him. "Because I have commitments on Friday evenings." He'd been going out every Friday night for how long? How had Mum forgotten? Regardless, he wanted to help. Somehow. "Could Jack give you a hand?"

Her expression fell as she leaned the trees against the car then crossed her arms. "You know he won't lift a finger."

"I'll have a chat with him," Dylan said. But when? Time was getting on, but he didn't want to leave Mum disappointed.

"He's not here," Mum said. "He sent me a text saying he was going out with that strange friend of his. Look, it doesn't matter. I'll sort something out for myself."

Before Dylan could reply, Mum turned on her heel and headed up the verandah steps. She disappeared inside, the screen door banging loudly behind her. Dylan exhaled heavily.

Mum had summed up Jack's friend right: strange. Curt was strange. He'd once tied up a maimed fox and shoved it in an elderly lady's mail box. A shudder ran through Dylan. He didn't like Curt and really didn't like Jack hanging out with him, but if he said anything, Jack would be even more determined to continue the friendship.

Dylan glanced again at the trees leaning against Mums' car, the open boot with the remnant of her pond idea, then over to his bike. He wanted to help, but he'd missed the gathering at Adam's last Friday night so he wanted to catch up with the boys at Jason's tonight. Decided, he turned to his bike and strode towards it. He'd already told Jason he'd be over, and the last thing he wanted was to go back on his word and come across as unreliable to his new teammates.

* * *

"Nice bike, man!" Jason said.

Dylan pulled his helmet off and dipped his head to acknowledge the compliment. Jason wasn't the only one eyeing his bike. A grin curled on his face as he shrugged out of his riding jacket. Would he ever get tired of the attention the bike got? Never.

Smoke billowed from the barbecue pit, and the scent of roasting lamb marinated in rosemary and mint floated temptingly upon the air. Dylan's stomach cramped with hunger as he approached his teammates and shook their hands. More complements about his bike followed. "Thanks, fellas. She took a long time to save for, but well worth it.""Is there a special woman who'd love to be on the back of that bike?"

A wry grin tickled Dylan's mouth at Daniel's words. "Ah, no comment."

Hoots and challenging remarks met his answer, and someone thrust a drink into his hand. He chuckled to himself, surprised at how at home he felt in the presence of these men that he hardly knew. Still, he wasn't about to repeat the mistake he'd made with Josh—revealing feelings for Lexi only to be required to make progress updates at each training sessions thereafter. No, that one he would keep to himself.

"Sorry, guys. There isn't a special woman. Well, apart from the bike, that is." After the laughter subsided, conversation moved off him and circulated easily amongst the group while they sipped their drinks and the fire popped and meat sizzled. Listening as each man spoke, rebutted, joked, jibbed, and riled, Dylan relaxed into the afternoon and laughed often at their candid manner with each other. Next year was going to be one he'd never forget, and he couldn't wait for the year to close and the new season to start.

# SIXTEEN

Dylan paused and huffed a deep breath. To his left and right were nine-foot leafy walls, towering above him at every turn. Was the secret to escaping a maze to follow the walls to the left or follow the walls to the right?

As laughter and conversations floated over head from somewhere outside the maze, Dylan decided to follow the paths to his right, hoping each turn he took would be the exit of this irritating maze.

Christmas breakup at Amaze fun park on the outskirts of town sounded like a great idea when Dave suggested it. Now, separated from his friends and finding it difficult to get out of the maze, Dylan wasn't so sure. While the youth were following a series of challenges throughout the park, the leaders were there to have fun themselves and to assist were needed. But what if one of the leaders needed assistance? Namely, himself. Not that he'd admit it.

Voices sounded close by, muffled by the thick hedge surrounding him.

He stopped. He knew those voices. Where were they coming from? To the left, up ahead. He broke into a run, zigzagging and sprinting, ducking and weaving through the endless corridors and archways. Puffed, he stopped in front of a yet another dead end.

This wasn't fun anymore. He turned back to look at the way he'd come. How had got separated? Nick had been talking about the New Year's party on the beach he'd been planning and making weird gestures with his left hand. That's when his friends had started disappearing…

The truth dawned: he was the butt of a joke.

"Nice play, Nick!" Dylan shouted, tilting his head upwards as if that would help the words travel over the giant hedge around him. He hung his hands off his hips and waited. If Nick was having a game with him, he'd—

"About time! I have to cough up five bucks now."

Laugher floated in the air, and Dylan turned and spirited towards the melodic sound, ducking around each left turn. Before he knew it, he burst through the maze and out onto the open lawn. An applause met his ears before he saw the source and turned slowly to look to his left.

"Well done, D. Tell me, at what stage did you realize we were all gone?" Nick asked, his voice dripped with mockery.

Dylan raised an eyebrow as he sized Nick up. He could charge the man and drop him or ignore the obvious bait Nick dangled in front of him. He chose the higher ground. "Pretty much after you were all gone," Dylan said in a matter-o-fact tone. "I was just interested in beating the maze, not what you guys were doing."

"I wasn't in on it," Hope said.

As Trent moved away from the group, Dylan caught the cynical grin forming on his face. "Come on, guys. Let's grab a bite to eat."

Dylan fell into step with Trent as he moved past him, but didn't enquire about the grin he wore. He knew Hope would have had part in the gag. Hope and Nick were as bad as each other, and he didn't need Trent to confirm that.

"You up for the New Year's party Nick is planning?" Dylan asked as they headed to the Amaze café for lunch. The summer sun was beating down over the fun park, and he rolled up the sleeves of his lightweight beige cotton shirt, regretting his decision to wear jeans.

"Yeah, it should be good. Going to bring my guitar, play a few songs by the bonfire." Trent said.

"Bringing a date?"

Trent coughed a laugh as though the suggestion took him by surprise. "No."

Still uncomfortable, Dylan flicked his collar up to keep the sun off his neck. "You answered that a bit too quick..."

"Look out!"

Dylan dropped to the ground and glanced over his shoulder. A tennis ball just missed his head and he ducked again. Trent overbalanced on his heels and fell back onto his rear. Lexi and Hope had flung themselves behind a large shrub while Nick stood in bold defiance of the coming ambush.

Dave, head back and chest heaving, ran ahead of the charging young people. He was waving them on, panting as he called out instructions. "It's Brandy; Ball Tiggy! Last man … standing … wins. Run!"

Without second thought, Dylan rose and sprinted across the open lawn towards the Chinese gardens. With its droopy willows, weeping cherries, bridges, and garden sculptures dotting the landscape, Dylan knew he'd gain the advantage if he could reach the gardens and if necessary, hide. Dylan ran down the arched walkway and out into the gardens, with a quick glance over his shoulder before he ducked under the wisteria. From his vantage point he could see the game in play and could see those unable to keep pace quickly dropping out. He couldn't see any of his fellow leaders. Who had the ball? Matt did. He followed the line of sight to find Matt's target—Hope, poorly hidden behind a rock wall, but unable to see what was coming. Wanting to protect her, he ran to a stumpy hedge then hurried towards her position, keeping low.

"Look out!" Nick shouted from somewhere nearby, and Dylan pulled up short. He heard a squeal followed by an irrepressible laugh which he knew was Hope. She must have been tagged. Then a grunt from someone else nearby as they got tagged. Nick's voice sounded in defeat but acknowledging the young teen of a good shot. Dylan snuck a peep over the hedge to see only a handful of youth running around and a multitude headed back to the café. The players were thinning out fast and his competitive side rose with the challenge.

As he crept back along the hedge, determined to be last man standing, he caught sight of Lexi racing through the ached walkway into the Chinese gardens with two teens in hot pursuit. He sprinted towards the adjacent sculptures and halted behind a large fountain. He peered around the side. Lexi had tucked herself under a bridge. She wasn't hidden enough. The two tailing her raced over the bridge then separated as they searched the garden. Once they disappeared, he scurried along the hedge, leapt over the bridge, and landed soundlessly beside her.

"Let's go." He snagged her arm before checking where the two teens had run to in their search for Lexi. She gasped and he turned back to her. "What? You ok?"

"When did the game turn so serious?" She said between puffs. Her face was flushed and glistened with sweat. He looked her in the eye and winked. "We can't have the kids beating us. We'd lose face."

Without waiting for comment, he hauled her to her feet and across the garden. Around a giant rectangular wooden sculpture encrusted with leadlight, over a bubbling creek and under a thick drooping willow, pulling her roughly behind him as he slid in under the heavy branches. He turned to ensure she was ok. Her smile was bright as she hunched under the limbs of the tree and pulled debris from her hair. He relaxed. She was ok, and they were well hidden.

Adrenaline still pumping, Dylan grinned back at her while Dave shouted for Trent to throw the ball somewhere close by. An echoing taunt came back from one of the young people, and Lexi tried to muffle a giggle. When she raised her head and looked back at him, Dylan noticed a forked stick spiking from the back of her head. He offered a lopsided smile as he reached over to remove it. "You look like a reindeer with that stick—"

Dylan's arm froze as Lexi suddenly cowered in front of him, face averted and eyes downcast. "Lex?" he asked, his voice hushed.

The silence between them lengthened as he watched the uneven rise and fall of her chest. The hand on her lap clenched into a tight ball and he wanted to reach out to her, to comfort her, but he heeded the voice of caution. He lowered his arm.

Lexi's breath came out as a shudder. "I'm … sorry," Lexi said. Her voice was distant and barely above a whisper.

"For what?" Dylan asked as gently and quietly as he could.

Footsteps splashed though the nearby shallow river, followed by what sounded like Dave's laughter as he was chased by the remaining youth. The sounds grated in harsh contrast to where Dylan found himself.

"Um, the doctor said this would happen …" Lexi still averted her face, but he could see her throat working. "He … he said I'd have flashbacks, but I didn't think they'd be so real."

The breath rushed out of Dylan and he sat back from her as the reality of what she'd said stuck home. He recalled the night he witnessed her assaulted by an ex-boyfriend. When she looked up at him, her blue eyes were haunted, and he inwardly cursed himself. If he could have a do-over, he'd never have left her side that night. He'd known Brad was trouble, and he'd never forgive himself for letting her out of his sight. He felt sick.

"The doctor said I'll get better. It'll just take time."

His jaw clenched as he realized something he'd done, reminded her of that night. Of Brad.

Lexi's hand unclenched as she relaxed ever so slightly. The rosy glow had faded from her complexion and she sat before him, pale and trembling.

"I … just need time," she whispered before her eyes flickered back to his.

Dylan understood what wasn't said and dipped his head. If time was what she needed, he would give her time.

# SEVENTEEN

A mild, cloudless evening settled over The Valley on New Year's Eve. The indigo sky was littered with stars, the perfect night for a party on the beach.

Dylan stood in front of his wardrobe, towel around his waist and ran a hand over his chest. The smell of cut hay from the neighbor's paddocks filled his room and he took a deep breath of the woody, earthy scent. The party was due to start in a little over an hour, but he was struggling with lack of motivation. He hadn't seen Lexi since the youth break-up. Christmas had come and gone since then, but their last interaction still sat like a lead weight in his guts.

She would be there tonight.

What would happen at midnight?

The house screen door banged shut. Moments later, a car spun its wheels on their gravel driveway then hurtled out the gate and down the road. Dylan sighed as he looked out his window after the car, two fading red lights disappearing fast. Jack becoming an odd mix of agoraphobic and socialite, another worry. Tonight the socialite side had reared its unpredictable head and he'd left their home with a group of young people Dylan hadn't seen before. After a prayer for Jack's safety, Dylan snagged a pair of white baggy surf-branded shorts, a black sleeveless shirt, and his trademark Havaianas, slung his beach bag over his shoulder and headed out of the house.

His spirits lifted the moment he pulled up his bike at the beach car park and saw the smoke of the bonfire blazing on the dunes with the sound of milling people rising with it. After removing his riding attire and locking the bike, Dylan strode down the sand towards his friends and grinned. Someone had strung up the volleyball net. If there was one thing he loved besides football, it was beach volleyball.

"Hey, big fella!"

"Josh." Dylan greeted his old teammate, firmly shaking his hand. "Good to see you."

"You too, bud. Up for a game?" Josh asked, passing the volleyball from hand to hand and gesturing with his head towards the net. "Got some tough competition lined up."

Dylan raised an eyebrow at Josh before checking out the competition. Lexi and Hope. As he watched Lexi use Hope for balance while stretching her quads, his mind returned to their awkward moment under the willow tree and found himself shaking his head. "Not right now, mate. Maybe after tea?"

Without waiting for an answer, he shouldered his bag further and continued to where Trent was manning the barbecue. Another time, a volleyball game would have been a great opportunity to break the ice, test the waters, and maybe flirt a little. But not now. Restless, he dumped his bag beside the beach barbecue site. "Hey, man. What's cooking?" Dylan asked Trent.

Trent glanced up at him as he turned the sausages. "The usual. Sausages, burgers, onions, potatoes, vegie patties. Why aren't you playing volleyball? I saw the net go up and thought you'd be the first to set the ball."

"Thought I might have something to eat first," Dylan said. A crowd began to gather down the shore from them. The banners going up around the party looked like the local radio station. Were they—

"Rubbish." Trent flipped the burger patties.

"What?"

"You expect me to believe that?" Trent said.

"Believe what?"

"That bull you just tried to feed me." Trent said placing the tongs down, he crossed his arms, and raised an eyebrow in a challenge for truth.

Dylan rolled his eyes. "All right. I'm not playing because Lexi's playing. Happy?"

Trent took a step towards him, his expression concerned. "Don't tell me it's over before it's even started."

Irritation curled in Dylan's stomach. "No. She wants time, so I'm giving her time."

The party down the beach was growing louder and larger by the minute, and the music was inviting. Dylan hated to think of leaving Nick's party, but anywhere less awkward right now was where he wanted to be. Trent's hand fell upon his shoulder, and he looked back at him.

"Fill me in here. I mean, I know something was different about you two after the youth break-up. Did something happen during the game?"

Dylan blew his breath out, then shared what had happened during the game. As he spoke, he felt his irritation grow to uncomfortable levels. It was almost hard to believe that just a few of months ago, he and Lexi were like best friends. Now some unspoken tension lay between them, and he wanted it gone. Needed it gone.

He missed his friend.

"Listen." Trent pinched the bridge of his nose in thought. "I agree there was a double meaning to what she said, but you can't avoid her. That would make things worse. Just be a friend. And, when ... if ... the good Lord deems something more should happen, it will happen."

"Yep. You're right." Dylan placed a hand on Trent's shoulder. "Thanks, mate. I'll be back for a feed shortly." Eager for distraction, Dylan moved away from his friend. The party setting up down the beach drew his attention once more as flashing lights began to flicker, and singing was emanating from the gathered crowd. While weighing up his options for evening, he noticed Nick jogging lazily towards him.

"Hey brother, you're not thinking of leaving the party, are ya?"

"I was considering it." Dylan shook Nick's hand.

Nick laughed. "Don't even think about it. It's going to be great here tonight. And midnight over in that camp won't be as exciting as midnight in our camp."

Dylan rolled his eyes at Nick's obvious suggestion and masked his annoyance with a chuckle. "Who do you have your eye on?"

Nick drew close and turned Dylan to face the bonfire blazing before the blackened waters of the ocean. With a quick flick of his head towards a group of young women dancing together by the large sound system he'd set up, he said. "See the brunette? Leggy, green halter-neck top, cut-off jeans?"

"Yeah," Dylan said. She wasn't the stand-out in the group, and he turned to Nick for verification, but Nick was still watching the girls.

"Her name is Alice," Nick said, looking back at him. "I met her at the police academy."

Dylan looked back at the girls. "Someone should warn her."

Nick shoved him down the sand dunes. Dylan caught himself, then circled back to his friend's side and laughed seeing the look of disgust angled towards him.

"She's into me, I'll have you know," Nick said.

Dylan held his hands up in gesture for peace, though he couldn't rein in his smile. "Then don't let me stop you, buddy. All power to ya."

Nick gave Dylan a suspicious second glance, then jogged towards the ladies on the beach. Dylan grinned when Alice greeted Nick with a lingering hug. If only Dylan's New Year's Eve could be as simple. Hunger gnawed at his stomach and he made his way over to Trent by the barbecue, reminded how hungry he was.

Two plates of food, a block of chocolate, two bananas, an apple, half a watermelon, and a bottle of water later, Dylan picked at the bag of grapes between him and Trent as they watched the volleyball. A crowd had gathered around the net as Josh and his teammate continued the match against Hope and Lexi. It was game for game, and neither side was backing down.

"Where's Nick?" Trent asked, keeping his gaze on the game.

Dylan cast a look over his shoulder to the shoreline and scanned the group dancing in the shallows. Neither Nick or Alice were among them. "I reckon he's gone for a walk."

"A walk?"

"Didn't you hear his plans?" Dylan turned to Trent in time to see him shake his head. "He's got his eye on a girl. Since they're both missing this close to midnight, I'd say he's ah … gone for a walk with her."

Trent turned back to the game, shaking his head. "What are your plans for midnight?"

The question Dylan was hoping to avoid. He cleared his throat. "No plans for me. I'm thinking I might take off."

Trent turned towards him, but he kept his eyes on the game. He wouldn't be talked into staying. Wouldn't encourage the expectations placed upon him when the clock struck midnight. He wanted to kiss Lexi, but a crowded beach party was not the right place. He turned his wrist over to check his watch. 11.42pm. He glanced at Trent and read the expression on his friends face. He wasn't going to argue. He reached a hand over himself to Trent, "Happy New Year, man."

Trent grasped his hand firmly. "Happy New Year."

# EIGHTEEN

With a final tug, Dylan pulled the bag straps on his Harley firm.

The night had gone pretty much as he'd expected, but he still felt disappointed. Leaving early was supposed to have removed the feeling of unfulfilled anticipation. He pulled his leather jacket on, then unclasped his helmet from the bike.

"Hey, where are you going?"

He looked up. Lexi was panting as she approached. She must have sprinted up the sand dunes to catch him. She stopped a few meters from him in the lamplit car park with her hands on her hips, her face flushed and eyes bright. "It's not midnight yet. You can't leave the party early."

Surprised, he placed the helmet on the seat and stepped around the bike towards her. "I'm a little tired, and not really in a party mood."

She swallowed, her breathing slowing. "So why'd you come?"

Dylan read the hidden question behind her eyes and felt a warmth lick up the back of his neck. They were alone and out of view of the party. "Nick would have been upset if I didn't put in an appearance."

"Of course," Lexi said, her gazing flitting from him to take in their surroundings. "Haven't got to talk to you much tonight. Do you have any New Year's resolutions?"

The din from the parties on the beach seemed to rise notably, and the whistle of a firecracker drew his attention in time to see it explode in brilliant pinks and blues against the night sky. "A couple. Mostly to excel at the Condors and try to look after the family. You?"

"I'm praying for some chances to do a bit public speaking next year. How I get there, I have no idea. I'm sure Toastmasters will work it out though."

Dylan dipped his head. "I'm sure they will. You'll be great, Lex."

Another explosion sounded, followed rapidly by what sounded like machine gun fire. The sky was illuminated with extraordinary color and the familiar shouts of well-wishing floated over the dunes towards them. It was midnight.

"Yeah, well … maybe," Lexi said. "I mean, my confidence isn't good at the best of times. But anyway, I never got to thank you for … that night. Things might have been different if you hadn't shown up."

Dylan blew his breath out and dropped his head. "Not soon enough."

When she didn't say anything, he raised his eyes to hers and saw a sadness in her expression he couldn't gauge.

"I hope you don't blame yourself for what happened," Lexi said quietly. "I mean, I should have done what you asked and not left the room with him. It's all my— "

"Don't say that. It wasn't your fault. It was Brad's fault." Dylan interrupted. Unwanted memories flooded his mind—the sickening blow Lexi had taken. Lexi falling to the ground. Lexi semi-conscious. All scenes he wished he could forget.

He would have ripped Brad apart if Trent hadn't pulled him away.

"Sorry." Lexi said took a step towards him. His body responded and he stood straighter, toying with his bike gloves.

"I'm off to training camp in January. I'm not sure where it will be yet."

"I know. Hope told me. Josh told her. So you won't be at church then?"

He shook his head. "Not for the month of January, anyway."

"We'll miss you."

His gaze locked on hers as more well-timed fireworks exploded in the sky behind her, illuminating her auburn hair a fiery array of reds. Any other woman standing before him, he'd wouldn't have wasted anytime in closing the distance between them and ceasing the conversation. But Lexi's words from ten days ago still rang in his ears.

She glanced over her shoulder, then shifted her weight. She looked like she wanted to say something, so he waited out the silence. When she looked back at him, he read the look in her eyes clearly. She gestured over her shoulder.

"Ok. Um. I better let you get going if you're tired. I'll head back to the party."

He dipped his head. "Ok."

Lexi didn't move. She tightened her ponytail, then brushed her fringe aside before glancing over her shoulder again. "Ok. Well, happy New Year then," Lexi said, her words rushed. "See you when I see you."

She turned away, and Dylan took a step towards her. "Lexi."

His chest tightened at the look on her face as she turned back to him. Her eyes were wide and searching as he took another step towards her. He sensed she was after reassurance as much as he, so he gently tipped her chin up and pressed a kiss to the corner of her mouth. Her soft intake of breath electrified every part of his body and he lingered, fighting the desire to cross the line she'd drawn.

Respect won over, and his hand slipped from her face as he took a step back and watched as she slowly opened her eyes.

"Happy New Year, Lexi."

# NINETEEN

The ground disappeared quickly beneath him as the thrust of the powerful Rolls-Royce engines lifted the A380 off of the tarmac and into the sky. Fascinated, Dylan took in all he could see out the small window beside him—the airport, the surrounding suburbs, The Valley. He watched as his hometown became a mere dot on the expanse of land below as the plane rose higher and higher. Cirrus clouds filled his view and he strained to see beyond them. Five minutes later, his view had transformed into a blanket of soft marshmallow with a brilliant blue dome. Disappointed to lose the view so early into the long flight, Dylan sat back in his seat and wondered how he was going to pass the seventeen-hour flight time to Arizona via Los Angeles. Not to mention how he would go altitude training for the first time.

"How are you enjoying your first flight?" Jason asked, a welcome interruption Dylan's line of thought.

He glanced at his teammate beside him. "It's not too bad, actually."

A chuckle from the seat in front of them drew his attention. Daniel turned to peer at him between the headrests. "You're only half an hour in. Let's see if you still hold that opinion in a few hours."

"How do you blokes pass the time?" Dylan asked, glancing around those tuning into their conversation.

"We solve the world's problems," Adam said from behind him.

"And each other's." Jason gestured for the flight attendant. "Wanna drink?"

"No thanks." Dylan listened the boys around him. Their conversations drifted from friendly banter to discussing world events, giving financial advice and—to Dylan's surprise—even a spiritual debate. Interested, he readjusted himself in his seat and wondered if he should input into the conversation or wait until someone asked for his opinion. Everyone was having their say, but something held him back.

He would wait.

If God wanted him to speak, someone would ask him a direct question.

Dale, who'd initiated the discussion, stood with a huff and made his way to the rear of the plane.

"Dale hates this conversation." Jason mumbled quietly to Dylan.

"If he wants to keep bringing it up, then he'll keep getting hammered." Tom waved a dismissive hand.

Dylan hadn't had much to do with Tom Mitchell, the teams powerfully built center forward with a jaw that could measure right angles. From watching the interactions of each man within the team, he pegged Tom as one of the influencers. A nudge within his conscious was felt and he frowned.

"He's just looking for opinions, Tom," Adam said. "No need to pounce on him for that."

Eyebrows raised, Tom pinned Adam with an expression Dylan imagined was usually reserved for grand finals. "I'm sorry, have we not discussed this before with him?"

"Yeah, but—"

"Then we don't need to discuss it again, do we?"

Surprised by Tom's attitude, Dylan found the words exiting his mouth before he thought them through. "Things are generally discussed until answers are found. If the topic keeps coming up, I guess you haven't answered his questions."

A silence fell over their group, but Dylan refused to look away from Tom's challenging glare.

"What's your opinion then, Dylan?" Daniel asked, swiveling in his seat.

"Well, you can't make a blanket statement that God doesn't exist because bad things happen to good people. Bad things happen to everybody, good and bad. It's the reality of the world we live in."

"Yeah, ok. I bet you're a creationist too," Tom said. A few of the others chuckled at Tom's mocking statement.

Dylan lifted a shoulder. "What's wrong with that?"

"Only the fact that the notion of an all-powerful, all-encompassing being creating things then leaving them to their own detriment is ridiculous."

Dylan glanced towards the rear of the plane to see Dale making his way back towards them. He wondered why Dale brought this, of all topics, up. It was clear this was not the first time this argument had been had, however it wasn't the time to ask Dale about it and play catchup. So, he decided to catch Dale by himself sometime over their trip and find out more about his teammate. He turned back to Tom, and grinned lopsidedly, "Tom, have you heard of Mount Rushmore?"

Tom looked back at him with a bored expression, and Dylan held his grin while waiting. He suspected Tom knew where he was going with the question, so he raised an eyebrow, daring him to answer.

"Of course I do. Everyone does."

"Should I ask you how it was made, or are you going to tell me it formed by chance?"

Chuckles reverberated softly around them while Dylan continued to hold Tom's attention. Tom mumbled something to the teammate next to him and sat back in his seat, and Dylan turned to look out the window. He'd made his point.

Jason elbowed him in the side.

"You've got guts, man. I hope that courage follows you onto the football field."

# TWENTY

"All right, lads. Welcome to the hardest two weeks of your life."

Nathan Carter, the renowned Condors coach, was not what Dylan was expecting. Though he'd watched the man on TV, he'd imaged him to be bigger, taller, broader. He'd expected more of a presence than the small-statured man addressing them as they filled off the plane in Phoenix.

Once in the boarding lounge, Dylan listened as his new coach barked out the fortnight's schedule. Were any of his sleep-deprived teammates listening? He wasn't. A sharp shoulder bump brought his wandering mind back in focus.

"Pay attention," Jason said, concealing his words in a cough.

A retort burned on his tongue, but Dylan kept silent. Judging by the short reproof he'd just received, Coach Carter was not a man to put up with anything less than undivided attention.

Tired and nursing a headache, Dylan followed his teammates onto the hired bus that would take them to the training camp grounds that would be their home for the next two weeks. Over the long plane flight, he'd listened to the boys swap stories of previous training camps and he'd stored away the advice they sent his way.

He had a feeling he was going to need it.

* * *

At the training camp, log cabins dotted a steep tree-filled hillside away from the mess hall and oval. As Dylan followed his teammates in silence up the stone track towards his quarters, he looked up at the silhouetted trees against the night sky. A cabin in the woods … Dylan's mind flashed back to the last horror film he'd watched—over five years ago, back when it was considered cool to scare yourself. Cool wasn't the word he'd use to describe how he was feeling now. While his body ached for a cozy bed and a good night sleep, the adrenaline starting to tense his muscles was not a good sign.

"Saunders. Room eighteen."

Coach Carter's voice drew him from his wayward thoughts, and he readjusted the bag over his shoulder as he stepped between his teammates. "Thanks, Coach."

A curt nod was his reply and Dylan moved towards the door of the cabin, glancing after the rest of the group as they disappeared into the blackness of the night.

The room was modestly furnished with a double bed flanked by two bedside tables, a couch off to his right next to a single window, and a very small bathroom to his left. He looked at his watch: quarter past two in the morning. Coach Carter wanted them at the oval at first light. So much for a good night's sleep.

\* \* \*

A sharp noise tore Dylan from his slumber. Disorientated, he bolted upright. His sluggish brain kicked in and he reached for the phone. Who would be messaging him at this hour? Annoyed that in his tiredness he hadn't set his phone to do-not-disturb, Dylan rubbed his eyes and looked at the home screen. A message from Trent flashed. He opened it.

*Nick got his police cadet placement in a city precinct. He's not happy. Say a prayer for him. Trent.*

With a heavy sigh, Dylan put his phone back on the bedside table and yawned. Not only had he just managed to get to sleep, but that was news he didn't want to receive and now his brain was in overdrive. Thankfully, he was in a room on his own and the message hadn't woken any other weary travelers. Should he message Trent back, reminding him of the time difference? No. Trent knew he was in the USA. He wouldn't have sent the message unless Nick really needed prayer cover.

Now.

Too weary to climb out of bed, Dylan stared up at the ceiling and, with his ears filled with the eerie calls of coyotes, lifted his friend up in prayer.

\* \* \*

The morning sun woke him before the knock on his door, and Dylan threw back the covers while mentally preparing himself for what he imagined was going to be a tough day.

As he made his way down the hill toward the oval, Dylan took in the sight of the countryside around him. Jagged peaks outlined against a cloudless cerulean sky and the clean-cut emerald-green lawns leading towards the main log cabin took his breath away. It was so different to The Valley back home.

"Good morning, Condors!" Coach Carter's voice rang out across the oval, echoing up the mountains behind them. "I trust you all slept well and are ready to get going. In case any of you missed what I said after we arrived, your days will be as follows: wake at six am. Breakfast at seven. Training from nine until twelve, then lunch. Training again from two until five. Dinner at seven. Then showers, massages, and downtime until lights out at ten-thirty. Any questions?"

Dylan glanced around at his teammates. They had a seasoned look about them and the schedule didn't make them blink, but this was going to be a large jump for him. Particularly the altitude training sessions. When they were dismissed to the hall for breakfast, Dylan quickly caught up with Jason and fell into step with him.

"Morning, Jace." Dylan used his best Coach Carter impression. "Are you refreshed and ready to go?"

Jason chuckled. "Are you kidding? I feel like I've been hit by a bus."

"Tell me something. Are these sessions really as bad as—"

"They're intense," Jason said as they reached the hall. "You'll be feeling it by the end of the day, and I wish I could tell you it gets easier."

The breakfast hall smelled deliciously of roasted coffee beans, hash browns, and frying mushrooms, but Dylan's eyes fell upon the fresh fruit platters and lemon water sitting on the tables. "I'm up for it."

Jason rapped him on the back as they entered the hall. "I'm sure you are. These two weeks bond us together as a team, and it's a privilege to train under the best."

As they sat at the table, they were joined by Adam and Dale. The rest of the team filed in, and the hall was soon filled with the sounds of clattering plates, chatter and laughter. All too soon Coach Carter called breakfast to a close and they were excused from the hall to start training.

# TWENTY-ONE

"*I* never thought it would hurt this much." Dylan said, his words muffled by the face hole of the massage table. His arms hung loosely off the table as the masseuse worked his strained hamstrings and calves.

Muffled chuckles sounded around him. "What did you think we were over here to do?" Adam asked in an amiable voice.

"This isn't local footy anymore, pup." Tom muttered.

Dylan frowned. If his gut was right, and it generally was, Tom was still annoyed about being challenged on the plane.

"Shall we discuss your first training camp Tom?" Daniel asked, silencing Tom.

Wincing as the masseuse worked the trigger points in his calves, Dylan chose not to respond to Tom's comment. Instead, he listened as the other men had their say.

"Tell the story, Cap," Jason said.

"Nobody needs embarrassing. Tom knows what happened," Daniel said.

"If he wants to dish it out, he's gotta take it," Adam said, a laugh in his tone.

"I know," Daniel said, grunting as the masseuse worked on him. "But this camp is about binding us together, not causing division."

"I'm just saying this isn't local football," Tom said, his tone contemptuous. "This is the big time, and he needs to bring it if he'll last."

At the masseuse's request, Dylan rolled to his back for the front of his legs to be worked. Though he had enjoyed the hard day of weights, ropes, and swimming, it was the cycling that had burned his legs and drained the last of his energy. Tomorrow would be more of the same, except altitude training would replace cycling in the afternoon. That part of the training had Dylan worried.

When the masseuse excused him, Dylan swung his legs off the table and walked from the massage room, surprisingly free of pain. His body felt like jelly, and his muscles were loose and relaxed.

"How do you feel?" Daniel asked, slapping him across the back as he fell into step beside him.

Dylan glanced at him and let out a relieved laugh. "Great, actually."

"They're fantastic at their work. They'll have you feeling one hundred per cent every night before bed."

The evening was warm but the breeze cool as they stepped from the treatment center.

"What do the boys do now?" Dylan asked as they crossed the lawn towards the stony path that would take them to their cabins.

"Most go to bed, but there are a few who stay up for a chat. You're welcome at my cabin if you're not ready to turn in."

"I'll have a shower first and see how I'm going. I might just want to hit the sack." Dylan had already decided he was headed for bed.

Daniel laughed as he veered off the path towards one of the first cabins. "Well, I'm in cabin three if you get your second wind."

With a wave, Dylan continued walking up the hill towards the bed he'd been desiring to fall back into since the sun woke him some sixteen hours earlier. Late night conversations with the boys would have to wait. As he approached his cabin, he noticed Dale leaning casually against one of the verandah posts, arms crossed as he looked over the valley below. If he'd noticed Dylan approaching, he didn't let on.

"Hey, Dale." Dylan dropped his sports bag on the ground outside the front door.

Dale turned with a casual air. "Saunders, you got a moment?"

"Sure. What's up?"

Dale made a gesture towards the cabin with a tip of his chin and Dylan, catching his meaning, moved towards the cabin door and pushed it open. "How about we chat inside? I need to put my feet up."

Once inside, Dylan flicked on a lamp and took a seat on the couch. When put his feet up on the coffee table, he expected Dale to do likewise, but the man seemed distracted. He paused in front of the window, studying the scenery same as before he asked to come inside. Dylan raised an eyebrow as he considered how to start the conversation. "So you're a Christian." Dale continued to look out the window.

Dylan pulled his legs back off the coffee table and sat forward on the couch, "Yeah. I am."

With one smooth and fluid movement, Dale moved from the window and sat down on the adjacent couch to Dylan. "Then perhaps you can answer a question for me."

"I'll do my best," Dylan said, mentally asking God for help. "Fire away."

The cabin fell quiet, and Dylan waited out his teammate. When Dale cleared his throat and raised his head, his dark eyes seemed to look right through Dylan.

"Maybe you can tell me why is that bad things continue to happen to good people if God is meant to be some all-mighty and all-powerful being?"

Dylan's eyebrows shot up as an exhale of surprise escaped him. He couldn't help his reaction. While he had hoped for an opportunity to speak with Dale about this very topic, he hadn't expected Dale to seek him out and bring it up so abruptly. Dylan rubbed his face as he sat back into the couch. This topic was hard enough when on top of your game, let alone when he was weary from a day's training. He cleared his throat. "That's a big question. Are you after a quick answer or something more substantial?"

Dale leaned forward in his seat. "I want an answer that makes sense."

"How are you with your basic laws of physics?" Dylan asked, muffling a yawn.

"What like, cause and effect?"

"Yeah," Dylan said. "Or good and bad." He watched Dale. He was either going to ask more questions, or he'd leave with something to think about. In the silence that followed, Dylan continued to silently asked God to direct the conversation and keep his mind sharp.

Dale's brow furrowed in thought. "You're saying good and bad exist in some directly proportional state?"

Dylan nodded, agreeing with Dale's statement. If he continued down this line, he'd figure out his own question and he could go to bed. His body was aching, and he had to be up at first light.

Dale sat back in his chair, gazing up at the thatch ceiling of the cabin. Dylan could almost see his mind turning over like a can of worms.

"Let's say good and evil exist like a basic law of physics," Dale said. "Tell me how it is that one of these laws seems to overpower the other. They can't be directly proportional if—"

"You just contradicted yourself." Dylan said, sitting forward on the couch. Slouching was making him sleepy, and Dale appeared to be here for the long haul. "It's not the law that's askew. It's your understanding of how the law works. There may appear to be an awful amount of bad happening in the world, but there is also a tremendous amount of good that goes on. How each good and bad impact on individuals is sometimes just luck of the draw, but sometimes it's self-imposed. But one doesn't overpower the other." He wouldn't mention the third option tonight—divine reasoning. Dylan stretched an arm over the back of his head as his muscles tightened up again. That subject would have to wait until Dale had this one under wraps.

"So why doesn't God stop bad things happening?" Dale asked. "If God is the all-powerful good in this scenario, he could stop it if he wanted to. Right?"

"He will stop it," Dylan said. "One day."

"And there's the brush-off answer," Dale said, his tone mocking as he looked away.

Dylan held back another threatening yawn and shook his head. "It's not a brush-off, mate. The two forces are at play against one another until everyone understands the full extent of the bad. Once we all recognize that, God will end it. You can take that to the bank."

Dale frowned. "Why won't he end it until then?"

"If He ends things before time, then you can bet bad will rise up again somewhere down the line bad, and the whole saga will start again. God doesn't want that to happen, so He has to let it play out for the ultimate good of all. The problem God has in this is you can't have love without freedom of choice. So He is waiting for everyone to make a choice for good or for bad. Once everyone has made their choice, then He'll end it. And not a moment before."

The cabin fell silent, and Dylan waited out his teammate. Outside, a scratching on the cabin door made the hairs on the back of his neck stand on end as a hooting owl flew past the window. If Dale was bothered by the nighttime noises in these woods, he didn't let on.

"You know," Dale said, voice hushed. "I think I understand what you're saying. It makes sense."

Dylan focused on Dale, while trying to ignore the continual scratching just outside the cabin. "Can I ask, why this question? The conversation on the plane gave me the impression this has been bugging you for a while."

"My little sister was diagnosed with cancer two years ago. She just turned seventeen."

Dylan nodded. "My dad died in a car accident four years ago."

"I'm sorry," Dale said.

The tone in Dale's voice and look of compassion on his face told Dylan he'd meant what he'd said. "I'm sorry about your sister, mate. I'll pray for her," Dylan said quietly.

"Thanks," Dale said. "And thanks for taking the time to explain this to me. I need a bit of time to think it over, but at the moment, it makes sense."

"Anytime you have a question, I'm more than happy to hear it," Dylan said.

Dale rose and extended his hand. "Thanks."

Dylan took his hand and shook it firmly. "Anytime."

# TWENTY-TWO

Dylan stood at the base of the incline before him and yawned.

Just jogging around base camp and exercising at 5,500 feet was hard enough for him. But over the last week, they'd begun exercising at 7,000 feet. He'd read about the science behind these training program and understood the goal of the trip was to gradually increase the altitude of training then maintain its effects back home using hypoxic chambers. Living it was a different story.

A shoulder bump jarred him. As he collected his footing in the scrub he looked after the familiar body jogging up the track.

"Get moving, Saunders!" Tom called over his shoulder as he disappeared around a bend in the track.

A grin tugged on Dylan's mouth as he considered Tom's attitude towards him. With a glance over his shoulder, he stepped back onto the track. He knew his comments to Tom on the flight over here hadn't been received well, but as long as Tom got it out of his system by game day, Dylan could handle him over training camp. Matter-of-fact, he'd help him.

After a few quick jumps on the spot to loosen his muscles, Dylan sprinted after Tom. A little competition never hurt anyone, and he smiled to himself thinking about Tom's face when he passed him and beat him back to camp.

The air was thinning. To draw a breath took twice the effort, and his lungs heaved as they worked to keep up with his brain demanding that his body keep moving. Tom was in sight. The crest of this track was in sight. His muscles burned, but not as much as the desire within him to show Tom what this pup could do.

"Get moving, Mitchell," Dylan said as he jogged past Tom. Only three words, but the effort to say them as if he was easily jogging their home ground took as much control as making sure he remained upright. He knew he was pushing past his limit, but something within him kept pushing him on. He had to make a point. He had to.

Dylan's lungs burned and his muscles felt like jelly as he started the descent. It was quicker than the rise, and he knew about two and a half kilometers would see him at an easier exercising level. He just had to make it. If he dropped now, he'd look like a fool.

Renewed energy swelled and pumped through his muscles.

* * *

The night was mild and still. Not a breath of wind blew, countless stars glittered above, and a hearty meal plus the evening massages had left Dylan feeling like he'd never felt before.

Wired.

He could almost run that track again. But for now, he'd settle for an easy walk back to his cabin and get some shut-eye. He couldn't stop imagining the look on Tom's face when he passed him at the crest. He chuckled to himself. They had another intense training session tomorrow, and the thought of outdoing Tom again made him grin. This year was going to be—

A firm hand fell upon his shoulder and turned him around. Eyes wide, Dylan looked back at Tom before his lopsided grin returned. He couldn't help his grin. Tom looked wild. He regained his posture and crossed his arms. "Evening, Tom. Great night out, isn't it?"

"You're a smug pup, aren't you?" Tom said, inches from Dylan's face.

Unruffled by the Tom's tone, Dylan looked him square in the face. "How about you stop calling me pup?"

"Would you prefer kid?"

A strange prickling tickled Dylan's skin and his grin tightened. He knew what Tom was trying to do and he was having no part of it. He turned to continue back to his cabin. Bed was calling. "No, mate. Just use my name or my surname. Thanks."

"You know, I was just like you when I started," Tom called out.

Dylan turned back to face him. "What?"

"You heard me." Tom moved towards him. "I was just like you. Talk of the football world and all that, but word of advice. It doesn't last. You get too far ahead of yourself and you'll wind up looking like a fool. So pull your head in."

Before Dylan could answer, Tom moved around him, deliberately bumping his shoulder as he passed. Dylan felt his jaw clench as he took a long breath in through his nose and turned. "I need to pull my head in? Do you hear yourself?"

Tom turned slowly. "I'm ten years your senior, kid. Watch it."

Dylan spat out a humorless laugh as he looked Tom over. The guy was serious. "With all due respect, I don't care how much senior you are." Dylan closed the distance between them. "I don't slam people for trying to get questions answered. I don't look to criticize other people's efforts, and I don't shove people off a running track. Out of the two of us, I'd say you're the one who needs to pull his head in."

When Tom didn't answer, Dylan let his words hang in the silence surrounding them. Not a breath of wind rustled the trees and not a cricket sang as Tom glared back at him. Somewhere deep inside, Dylan questioned himself as he held Tom's gaze. He was new at the club, and Tom was a seasoned player.

He should have held his tongue.

Just as disappointment in himself began to settle in and an apology started to take form in his mind, Tom's steel expression melted into an easy-going grin and he laid a hand on Dylan's shoulder. "You know, not one new recruit has ever stood up to me." He chuckled. "I'm impressed."

"What?" Dylan asked.

"Let's just say, I like to apply a little pressure to the new recruits to see what they're made of. You know, playing at our level isn't a walk in the park."

Dylan felt his face contort as he listened to Tom. He blinked. "So whatever this is has just been some form of … what? A test?"

Tom laughed as he draped an arm over Dylan's shoulder and steered him towards their cabins. "Surely you've heard of initiations, Dylan?"

"Well, yeah, but …." What was going on?

"Then I'm sure you didn't think you'd start your career with us without some form of initiation? It's good to see a bit of mongrel in you. You'll need on game days."

As they drew near to Dylan's cabin, Dylan turned out from under Tom's arm and looked back at his teammate. "I guess we're cool then?"

When Tom held his hand out, Dylan stared at it for a moment before clasping it. He still wasn't sure if he could trust the sudden change in Tom's demeanor, but he didn't want trouble with any of his new teammates. He wanted to enjoy the rest of the camp and play football.

"Of course, we are," Tom said. "Just remember, I'm still your senior."

# TWENTY-THREE

With heavy footfalls, Dylan climbed the verandah steps and moved towards the front door of his family home. Never had he been so happy to see the place.

Jet-lagged and physically exhausted, he unlocked the front door, closed it with his foot, and headed straight for his room. He knew he was meant to try and stay awake, but even Lexi's strongest espresso wouldn't keep his eyes open any longer.

\* \* \*

"Hey, bro. Bro! Wake up."

"What?" Dylan asked, his sleepy voice croaky and tipped with irritation. What was Jack doing in his room?

"Check this out!"

"That requires opening my eyes, something I'm not about to do." With a deep sigh, Dylan rolled onto his side away from his brother. He actually wasn't sure if he could open his eyes, even if he wanted to.

"Come on, Dylan. How often do I come in here or even care?"

He was right. Whatever Jack wanted to show him had to be good if he was showing interest in something outside of himself. "What time is it?" Dylan asked.

"Just after ten, Saturday morning. You've been asleep for ages. Look!"Just after ten. Church started at eleven. Even if he made it to church on time, he'd probably fall asleep during the service. Dylan pushed himself up with a grunt. "I gotta get ready for church."

"Church can wait. Look."

Dylan swung his legs off the edge of his bed and prepared for the head rush that would await him standing. "I have my priorities in order, Jack."

A newspaper landed beside him as Jack turned to leave the room. "Priorities smiorities. I just wanted to show you that."

With half interest Dylan turned to the paper lying crumpled beside him. Yawning, he scooped it up and looked over the front page. Seeing nothing of interest, he turned the paper over to look at the back page and froze.

There he was.

Jogging a track at 10,500 feet—the track he hated most—at the training camp he'd just returned home from. He gazed at the photo, thankful for the cap and sunglasses that hid his bloodshot eyes and sleep-deprived features. The headline, New Condor Flies High' brought a grin to his face, and he flipped through the paper to find the full article.

Paragraph after paragraph full of praise and predictions of future stardom brought a shine to Dylan's eyes. His back straightened as sense of pride tingled his nerve endings. He dropped the paper to his lap. He was reading about himself. In the statewide newspaper. With a shake of his head, he looked at the paper once more and laughed. Him!

His phone beeped from his bedside table, and he felt for it, unable to tear his eyes from the newspaper laying open on his lap. He pulled the phone close and saw a message from Nick flashing on the home screen. He opened it.

*'Welcome home Star. See you on the back page of the paper. Nice. Coming to our humble church this morning?'*

Church! Right. Dylan cast the newspaper aside and moved to the bathroom to shower and get ready. The clock in the bathroom read 10.42am. He was going to be late.

Twenty minutes later, dressed in a short-sleeved blue checked shirt and distressed jeans, Dylan made his way into The Valley church and slipped quietly into the congregation. He could see his friends seated towards the front, and Trent was with the band, his acoustic guitar resting over one knee while he watched the minister speak. Not wanting to interrupt the service, Dylan tried to focus. As he'd suspected, he began to feel a tiredness creep up on him the longer he remained seated.

*Must stay awake. Must stay awake.*

The minister's voice droned through his foggy mind. He loved Pastor Walker's services. Every week he left feeling inspired and challenged, so perhaps he was still feeling jet-lagged. Perhaps that was why his head felt like a bowling ball and his eyes burned with desire to close. Desperate to keep his eyes open, Dylan pulled out his phone and tried to take notes, but found himself taking longer blinks than necessary. He switched to checking his new club's website. The team photos had been taken before they headed to training camp, and he wanted to see if his profile was uploaded yet.

"Hey, you, is that church related?"

He started at Lexi's hushed voice beside him and flipped the phone over on his lap as he turned to greet her. The tiredness that had almost engulfed him vanished at the sight of her. "Not exactly."

She crouched in the aisle beside him, looking up at him with those azure-blue eyes that told him he was busted. A slight grin played upon her mouth, and Dylan found himself grinning back at her. "I was trying to stay awake. I'm still jet-lagged."

"Then why did you come to church?" Lexi asked.

*To see you.* Dylan felt his grin slip away at the rawness of the thought that flashed through his mind. He continued to hold her gaze. She blinked, cleared her throat then rose slowly. "Are you staying for lunch?"

There was a quiver in her voice and he dipped his head. "Sure."

"See you then. I'm going to help set up."

Once the final hymn was sung and benediction said, Dylan remained standing while Pastor Walker and the ministry team filed out. He caught Trent's eye and lifted his chin in greeting. Trent smiled warmly back.

It felt like ages since he'd last seen his friends.

Not long after, Dylan crossed the lush expanse of church lawn towards the picnic rug Hope had set up. The purple flowers from the jacaranda trees lining the church boundaries caught his eye and Dylan smiled. After spending two weeks in the rugged mountains of Arizona, being back in the green undulating hills of The Valley was like breathing fresh air.

"There he is!"

Hearing Nick call out to him, Dylan tore his gaze from the green surrounding him to the picnic blanket. "Hey, guys." He greeted Nick with a firm handshake before taking the plate of food Lexi offered him.

"Saw you in the paper, Saunders," Hope settled herself on the picnic blanket, "Can we say we know a celebrity yet?"

"Wait until he kicks his first goal," Trent said, his tone dry as he slapped Dylan on the shoulder before sitting next to Hope.

"If he kicks a goal." Nick raised a skeptical eyebrow and pointed a food-laden fork at Trent.

Dylan cleared his throat and looked pointedly at Nick. "When I kick that first goal, Hope, then you can say you know a celebrity."

Hoots and cheers echoed around him and Dylan felt his cheeks flame as Nick gestured with his hands an expanding action around his head. He gave Nick a playful shove, and then laughed. He turned his attention to the plate of food in his hand. Seeing himself in the paper this morning had taken him to cloud nine, and he wouldn't let anyone take that from him.

As he seated himself on the picnic blanket, he looked over at Trent, who chuckled while he gathered another forkful of food from his plate.

"Better watch that pride doesn't trip you over," Trent said quietly before turning his piercing green eyes to lock on him. "Pride comes before the fall."

# TWENTY-FOUR

The pre-season and premiership-season timetables Dylan was handed at the Condors first club meeting of the year was full on. He could see most of his week being swallowed up with the training alone, but there were also evening commitments and interviews, not to mention playing in the scheduled pre-season matches. As the intensity of the program sunk in, he felt a nudge in his side and turned to see Adam leaning towards him, eyes upon his own schedule. "It's full on, aye. Is your head spinning yet?"

"Tell me about it," Dylan's eyes travelled over the timetable, the enormity of the year ahead began to settle into his gut.

"Every year I look at this and think, how am I going to fit all this in plus time with my family?"

"I'll have to quit the leadership team." Dylan lay the timetable down and looked out the clubroom windows; the status he'd suddenly acquired was going to come at an uncomfortable price.

Adam turned to look at him. "What's that?"

Dylan shook his head and picked the timetable up again. "A program at my church. This has been so unexpected that I haven't had much time to gather my thoughts."

Adam laid a hand on his shoulder. "Might want to have a talk with those you do the leadership team program with soon as you can," Adam said. "Things are going to get hectic from now on."

Though Dylan knew Adam was referring to the football year, it also applied to other areas in his life. Namely, Jack.

Dylan had sensed something amiss since he'd returned home. Something was wrong, like the prickling sensation of the hairs on the back of your neck standing to attention when the phone rings in the middle of the night, or when the dog that never barks starts barking. Something wasn't right, and neither Mum nor Jack were giving any hint as to what it might be.

Once dismissed from the clubrooms, Dylan avoided small talk with the boys and headed for his bike. An urgency to get home had begun pulsating through his veins the moment Jack flashed into his mind.

"Hey, Saunders!" Daniel called.

With an iron-like will, Dylan suppressed his frustration at being stalled and turned at his captain's call. Daniel strode towards him, sports bag slung over one shoulder and drink bottle firmly in his grasp. "Will we see you Friday night?"

Friday night? Dylan searched his mind. The socials. "Yeah, sure. I'll be there."

"Good. I know this all landed on you pretty quick and people tend to book up towards the end of the year, but I hope to see you at the Friday socials now we've started a new year."

Translation: I expect you to be there.

"Yeah, she's cool, Cap. I'll be there." Even as he said the words, Dylan could hear the disapproving comments and visualize the saddened faces of those he shared—used to share—Friday night with once they heard he'd no longer be joining them. "Whose place are we meeting at?"

"Jason's. Beware, his dog is vicious." Daniel laughed as he slapped Dylan on the back before he turned to leave. "See you there."

Dylan looked after his captain for a moment before turning back to his bike. "Yeah. See you there."

* * *

Upon arriving home, nothing grabbed Dylan as out of the ordinary.

Jack was watching another police show on TV, and Mum was fussing over her recipe book in the kitchen. Still, something felt different. With a quick hello, he strode to his room, dumped his sports bag on the floor of his room, and headed back outside.

Outside, everything was the same. He rubbed the stubble forming on his chin and looked left then right, taking in the lengthening shadows of the day and the pink-orange hues in the clouds above, then jogged down the verandah steps. He'd prayer walk the house, their property boundary, then the block. While he couldn't see it or hear what had ruffled him, God knew.

It was dark by the time he returned home. The prayer walk had taken longer than he thought, but pouring his heart out to the Lord above had lightened his spirit so much that he'd done two laps of the block. As he approached the house once more, he felt the Lord's protection. The dark clouds that had seemingly settled over them were now gone. A fresh air surrounded the house, and Dylan breathed deeply of the Lord's presence.

Inside, the lounge room was completely dark. The flickering light from the TV could usually be seen, illuminating the room at haphazard intervals. He frowned as he jogged up the front steps and pulled open the screen door. The house was quiet, and he stepped quietly into the kitchen where Mum was seated at the table, a cup of coffee cooling beside her.

"Mum?"

She looked up. Her body seemed to respond to him before her mind did, and a moment passed before she blinked and greeted him with a tired smile. "Hi, sweetie. How was your day?"

He pulled a seat out and sat. There was a ring of condensation on the table under her cup. How long had it been sitting there, untouched?

"It was good. The meeting was interesting, and I got my timetable for the year. It's going to be busy."

She nodded. A sad look flashed through her eyes before she averted her gaze to the coffee cup.

"Want me to make you another cup?" Dylan asked. He couldn't tell what mood he sensed coming from her, but he wished she'd spill whatever was upsetting her.

She shook her head and looked back at him, "No. I didn't want it. I just made it out of habit."

"Where's Jack?"

Another flash of sadness in her eyes. "Dunno. He came in here about a half hour ago, restless. Asked where tea was. When

I said I hadn't prepared anything yet, he shouted horrible things, knocked a chair over, and left."

Dylan shifted forward in his seat. Concern and fury met uncomfortably in his mind. He'd never seen Jack behave the way Mum sometimes described, but he didn't doubt what she said. He knew Jack wouldn't be bold enough to pull those stunts with him, and it bothered him that he would be like that with Mum. "I'll wait up and talk with him when he gets back."

Mum pushed her chair back and rose. "Ok, sweetie. Goodnight."

Breathing a heavy sigh, Dylan slid deeper into his chair and rapped his fingers on the kitchen table. Mum still hadn't prepared anything for tea. It was after half past nine. Toast for tea it was, then he'd wait for Jack to show himself.

"God help me," he said. The quietness of the house swallowed up his words, as a feeling of dread curled in his gut.

# TWENTY-FIVE

Dylan looked at his watch. 4:12 a.m. Jack still wasn't home.

He'd been waiting for Jack since Mum went to bed. Waiting in the dark, so as to not tip Jack off. Waiting, and trying not to fall asleep himself. Wherever Jack had gone, it was clear he wouldn't return home until he felt like it.

Another character trait Dylan didn't like.

He rubbed his face, slapped his cheeks, shook his head, and cracked his neck. "Come on, Saunders. Don't bail now. He'll be home soon."

As if he'd predicted it, a crunching of car tires sounded moments before the lounge room was briefly illuminated as a car's headlights grazed the front of the house. Dylan rose slowly and stepped towards the window.

Ever so slightly, he cracked a gap between the aluminum venetian blinds and watched as Jack and the driver exited the sleek vehicle. He could hear indistinct conversation. The driver lit up a cigarette, but it was too dark to make out the man's features, and the solar lights Mum had put everywhere around the house didn't offer much help. The driver handed Jack a piece of paper, then drew him into a bro hug. Dylan squinted against the dim light to see where Jack put the piece of paper as the driver got back in the car and drove it slowly down the drive. As Jack turned back towards the house, he slipped the paper into a back pocket.

Planning to confront his brother, Dylan moved to step into the hallway, when a thought flashed through his mind.

*Not tonight.*

Dylan halted. Jack's key found the lock, and the door latch clicked. A creak echoed through their home as the door swung open, and Jack's shadow filled the central hallway.

With quiet steps, Dylan slipped into the corner of the darkened lounge room. Obedient to the inner voice cautioning him against talking with Jack tonight, Dylan watched as Jack's long shadow disappeared as he closed of front door.

Prayers filled Dylan's mind for his little brother as Jack shuffled down the hallway. His bedroom door opened and closed.

Where had he gone and who was that driver? More importantly, what was on that piece of paper?

Exhausted, Dylan waited another couple of minutes before quietly heading down the hall to his own room. He would talk to Jack in the morning.

\* \* \*

Dylan woke with the loud crack of the screen door slamming shut against its frame, and groaned. He needed to fix the closer on that door. Birdsong outside his bedroom window filled the silence that followed, and Dylan peeled an eye open to check his bedside clock.

10:07 a.m.

Both eyes shot open. He threw back the covers and launched himself from the bed, and snagged his phone.

With heavy footfalls, Dylan strode down the hallway towards the kitchen, checking his phone as he went. Yep, he'd slept through the alarm, three missed calls, and two messages. He was supposed to be at training at nine. What a way to start the new year at the new club. He dialed Daniel back while concocting a number of excuses he could use to explain himself, but when his captain's voice came down the line, the excuses disappeared from his mind. "Cap, I am sorry. I have no excuse—just slept through my alarm."

"Least it's not game day." Daniel's tone was light.

Dylan's breath rushed out with relief. "Ha. From now on, I'll set two alarms. I've never slept through my alarm before. I was just about to grab my gear and head in."

"Cool your heels, big fella. I know the schedule says it's a training day, but I was actually calling to let you know we've cancelled training today. I couldn't raise you last night, so was actually a little relieved when you didn't rock up."

Dylan looked at this call log. Two of the missed calls were from last night while he was waiting for Jack to come home. "So what's on for today?"

"Enjoy a lazy one. It'll get busy from now on. Have a good one."

Dylan ended the call and placed his phone on the bench. The house was quiet, and the remnants around the kitchen told Dylan Mum and Jack had both had breakfast and left the house. He opened the fridge and took out a bottle of grape juice, chugging it down in one gulp. What would he do? If the year was about to get "mighty busy", then today he needed to catch up on odd jobs. He looked out the window and rubbed a hand up and down his bare chest, thinking. Where should he start?

Hours later, Dylan sat on the porch swing mentally ticking off the jobs he'd done and the ones he still had to do. Deep in his mind adrenaline was gearing up for when he saw Jack. The longer he stayed away, the more Dylan felt himself tensing up.

A car approached, and Dylan turned his attention to the driveway to see it was Mum's car. With Jack in the passenger seat. Where had they gone together?

"Good morning, sleepyhead," Mum called out as she exited the car. Dylan acknowledged her while keeping his eyes on Jack, who pulled his cap down and made his way inside as if Dylan wasn't there. Anger bubbled within Dylan as adrenaline pooled in his gut.

"When did you get up?" Mum's chirpy voice broke into his thoughts. He looked at her, as she waited by the front door for him to answer. Did she not notice Jack's attitude? "A little after ten. Where did you two go?"

"Oh, Jack took me out for a brunch date and some shopping. Said he felt bad about how he behaved last night. It was nice. Thank you for talking to him!"

Dylan blinked as Mum disappeared back inside the house. Jack took Mum for brunch? That was out of character, but this wasn't the time to attempt a conversation. He would grab him for a chat when Mum wasn't around. Dylan pushed himself off the porch swing and made his way to the garage to work on his bike.

Half hour later, sprawled on the patchy grass outside the garage, Dylan dropped the oil out of his bike and looked up at the sky while he waited for the oil to drain. There was something amiss, although he couldn't put a finger on what. His phone beeped from the work bench, and Dylan got up to retrieve it. A message from Dave flashed on the screen.

*Hi all. Well, it's February already! First Leadership Team meeting for the year starts tonight (sorry, had to be Tuesday this week. Will go back to Mondays from next week). At 8 pm instead of 7:30 pm. Bring your Bibles. Dave.*

A heaviness form within his mind as he considered his commitments with youth at church along with Daniel's earlier warning. It wasn't just Friday night youth group he'd have to let go. It was the whole Leadership Program.

Why delay the inevitable? Why commit to something he knew deep down was not feasible?

He slumped against his bike, clasped his hands at the back of his neck and groaned.

He had to talk to Dave.

# TWENTY-SIX

"Dylan!" Dave glanced back into his house before stepping out onto the porch and closing the door behind him. "I wasn't expecting you guys until eight. Aren't you working today?"

"Not today. Do you have a sec?" Dylan asked, his voice hushed. Dave looked at his watch. "I have a client here for counselling right now, and I'm fully booked for the rest of the day which is why I needed to move our LT meeting back a little. Is everything ok?"

There was no getting around what he had to do, and it would be easier letting Dave know now rather than in the middle of the meeting tonight.

Dylan cleared his throat. "My commitments with AFL are such that I won't have time for anything else this year. I've resigned from my job at the garage, and I'm here to do the same with the LT."

Dave's eyebrows rose to new heights and an uncomfortable silence followed. He waited Dave out, expecting the man would need a moment to process the news.

"Well, I wasn't expecting that," Dave said, widening his stance and crossing his arms.

Dylan felt himself waver. Resigning didn't feel right, yet here he was. Quitting his job at the garage had lifted a weight from his back, but pulling away from Youth felt different, as if a light had gone out in his spirit and he'd entered a dark place. He needed to do this, or he'd be setting the leadership team up for constant let-downs. He could not and would not do that.

"I'm sorry, Dave. I got my schedule from the Condors yesterday, and I'm expected to attend Friday night teambuilding sessions when we aren't playing games or traveling interstate. With all the training, meetings, and social functions, I can't see myself being able to fit anything else in. And I won't let you guys down by bailing on you last minute."

The door behind Dave creaked open, and an older man peered out at him. Dave turned and stepped towards the door.

"I'm sorry, Mr. Johnston. I'll be back in just a moment," Dave said. Dylan turned and took a few steps away from the house, feeling awkward at having interrupted a counselling session. He waited until he heard the door close before turning back to Dave.

"Dylan, I can't talk right now but I want to talk to you about this," Dave said. "When are you free?"

"I don't know, but can I give you a call when I get into the new routine?"

"Good. Do that. We'll arrange to catch up then. Are you going to tell the others?"

"Of course." He'd never consider asking someone else to do his business.

"Ok." Dave breathed a heavy sigh. "We can talk more later. Until then, keep in touch with God and don't live faster than your guardian angel can fly."

The look in Dave's eyes was intense as Dylan shook his out-stretched hand. There was more the man wanted to say, but time wouldn't allow.

However, Dylan was sure he already knew what that would be.

\* \* \*

Dylan sat on the balcony of The Mariners Inn, signaled the waiter, and turned his attention back to the murky blackness of the ocean. He rocked back on his chair and watched the gentle lapping of the water against the lamp-lit sand. It felt wrong to be here, waiting for his friends to finish up at the meeting at Dave's place when he should be at the meeting. But what was the point of being there if he wasn't going to be a part of the team anymore?

The evening sky clouded over to the point where the sky wasn't distinguishable from the ocean. It was just a picture of blackness before him, matching his mood.

"Here you go, sir. Can I get you anything else?" The waiter appeared beside him.

With a shake of his head, Dylan took the decaf chai the waiter had brought and turned back to look over the view. Daniel had told him that adjusting to a life in the spotlight would require sacrifices, but the sacrifice was worth it. It would have to be. If today was anything to measure by …

"So where were you tonight?" Trent's voice came from behind him.

Dylan rocked the chair back to four legs and turned to greet his friend. The others wouldn't be far behind. "Hey, man. How's it going?"

"By the look of you, I'd say better than you're going."

As Trent pulled up a seat beside him and turned his gaze out over the beach, Dylan took a long sip of his drink. Trent wouldn't push for details. He sighed. "I've got a lot on my mind."

Hope's laugh seemed to fill the upper room, and Dylan looked over his shoulder to see Hope and Lexi spill over the top of the stairs, laughing as they glanced back down the stairs. Nick emerged behind them, a lopsided grin on his face.

"Dylan. We missed you tonight." Hope stopped at the balcony edge and peered down to the footpath below. "You know, I've never been up here before. I've always eaten downstairs."

"We'll have to bring you here for your birthday." Lexi came to stand beside Hope, though she turned her back to the view and rested against the railing. "Unless Josh has organized something?"

Hope giggled. "He better have."

A hand clamped on his shoulder and Dylan glanced up at Nick. "We missed you tonight, brother. We will definitely need your height at youth on Friday."

Hope laughed, and pulled a chair up to Dylan's table. "Dylan, he's not kidding. Dave has us doing this—"

"I'm quitting the LT." Dylan said, his voice flat. He hated cutting off Hope's story, but he didn't have room in his head for idle chatter.

"You're quitting, or you've already quit?" Trent asked.

"Already have," Dylan answered, turning to look at him. "Spoke to Dave earlier today."

"So that's why you didn't come tonight?" Lexi asked quietly.

Dylan turned his eyes to her and toyed with his glass on the table beside him. Lexi's eyes flickered, betraying thoughts she no doubt intended to hide.

"I'm sorry." He spoke only to her.

"The first bounce of the season hasn't happened yet, and he's already acting like he's too good for us."

"Nick …" Trent said, a subtle warning in his tone.

Dylan tore his gaze away from Lexi and looked at Nick with measured patience. Nick raised an eyebrow at him. "It's not that at all."

"Turn it around then, star." Nick sat down heavily on a chair at a different table. "You're in our place. What would you say?"

"First you'd ask him why," Hope said.

"That's not how it is, Nick. Settle down a bit," Dylan said at the same time. He gave a quick glance at Hope.

Nick's expression was like steel, and Dylan met Nick's gaze with one of his own. "I didn't wake up this morning thinking I'll quit on my friends and leave them hanging. My hand has been forced."

"No one can make you do anything." Nick looked out over the ocean and shook his head. "You've made a decision and executed it without speaking to those it directly affects. Simple."

Dylan's eyebrows shot up; he thought his friend knew him better than that. He sat forward in his seat, ready to meet Nick head on, but he felt Trent's hand on his chest and allowed himself to be eased back into the chair.

"Nick," Trent said, "We all know Dylan's world has been turned on its head in the last two months. How about we support him instead of criticizing any decisions he makes based on his new reality?"

Nick didn't answer.

"What's changed since the last time we saw you?" Lexi asked.

"Nick's right—I should have spoken to you guys first." Dylan rubbed his eyes. He was so tired they were starting to sting. "I had a meeting at the Condors yesterday, and was given the schedule for the year. Its huge, guys. I find I'm expected to be present for club business on Friday nights when we're not playing or traveling. At first, I thought it was optional, but it's considered team building activities." He put a hand over his mouth to cover a yawn. "Then I got home to find Jack is up to no good, so I didn't get a wink of sleep all night. Got up this morning, got the text from Dave, and it hit me. I'll need to step down from the LT now too."

"That's … unexpected," Trent's quiet words summed up the mood of all in that moment. Dylan rubbed his face, his voice like gravel when he spoke. "I know I dropped this like a bomb on you guys. It's possibly because I've had twenty-four hours from hell. I've had no sleep, so I'm not thinking as clearly as usual, but it doesn't change the way things are now."

There was silence.

Somewhere beneath the balcony of The Mariners Inn, the noises of the road and nature strip rose up and filled the air around them. Never had it been so quiet while the five of them were together. Dylan stared at his empty mug. He was the reason behind the awkward silence. First with Lexi, now with the rest of them.

Maybe this split was a good thing.

The silence lengthened, and a sensation of not belonging set-tled over him. He shifted uncomfortably in his chair, surprised a thought like that would enter his mind, and lifted his gaze from the empty mug to encounter Lexi and Hope's awkward but smil-ing faces. He wished he could think of something to say.

"Well, I'm not sure what's more weird right now," Hope said. "Our team facing a split, or the fact we're all in the one room and it's quiet."

Dylan chuckled, thankful to Hope for breaking the tension. Lexi pulled a chair up at his table. "I'm pretty sure it's the sec-ond. I'm also pretty sure we're all a little shocked, but I know everything will be fine." Dylan felt a rap on his thigh and tore his gaze from the assurance that glowed in Lexi's expression, and turned to Trent.

"Whatever happens, we know God makes all things happen for our good and His glory. That's what we need to remember."

Dylan knew that promise well. In fact, he had both hands firm on that promise, no matter how hard things were to move forward, he would; and he would hold God to His word.

# TWENTY-SEVEN

Dylan had watched the Condors train, but he'd never imagined that one day he'd be training with them. Preparing to run out onto the ground with them. Playing to win with them. A wry grin formed on his face as he jogged lazily around the ground, bouncing the ball every few lengths, warming up with his new team.

"Saunders, pass it here." Dale appeared on his left.

Without hesitation, Dylan handballed to Dale.

"You ready for your first match?"

In just two days, Dylan would be running out to play his first professional game of AFL. He chuckled as he grasped the football Dale handballed back to him and bounced it. "I can scarcely believe it, but yeah I'm ready. Bring it on."

"The Southern Devils are a good team, and you're up against one of their most seasoned players."

Dylan glanced at Dale. "I was surprised to be matched up with Rick Hance, but figured Coach is testing me out."

"Shutting Hance down will be tough."

"You're telling me," Dylan said, handballing the ball back to Dale. A group of young kids running to the boundary line ahead caught his attention, and he watched as they waved Condor guernseys and pictures over their heads.

"Twenty-seven! Sign my top?"

"Over here, over here!"

"Dylan!"

"He looked at us, did you see?"

"Dylan!"

Dylan squinted behind his sunglasses and saw they were waving his number on the back of the guernseys and his picture from the newspaper.

"Looks like you've got a fan base already," Dale said, his tone light.

Dylan looked at Dale and raised his eyebrows, feeling a little embarrassed but strangely energized by their attention. He gave the kids a wave.

"Do you guys stop and sign things or just say hello as you pass?" Dylan asked.

Dale laughed. "Go sign what they've brought and make their day. Catch you out in the middle."

Time disappeared as Dylan took time out on the boundary line. He signed everything they handed over to him, careful to use his game autograph and not his actual signature, and posed for selfies with the kids. Sure he was going to wake up from a dream at any moment, he tried to keep himself grounded and enjoy the moment. However, there were so many kids vying for his attention and falling over themselves to get to him, his spirits soared higher than the towering flood lights above.

\* \* \*

It was unbelievable. He still couldn't believe it.

Though he'd done the training, been to the meetings, completed all the necessary pre-game preparations, it still hadn't sunk in.

The crowd roared above him, the sound like rumbling thunder reverberating through every fiber of his being, while the sunlight spilling down the race invited him to sneak a look outside. But he wouldn't. He had to stay focused, focus on the opponent he'd be up against in little under an hour, not the nerves. He felt as if he was going to throw up.

Coach Carter's voice boomed through the rooms, calling the team to focus on him, and Dylan snapped to attention. All restlessness vanished as he focused on the whiteboard in Coach's hand. Although this was only a February pre-season game, they were to play as if it was the premiership season that started in March: hungry. He looked around. He'd watched this team on TV for years. He'd followed them in the newspapers for years. He knew all the men's stats, their strengths, their weaknesses—

"Saunders!"

Dylan snapped to attention. "Coach?"

"You've done your homework on Hance?"

"Yes, sir."

"Keep close to him, but don't wear yourself out. Keep him thinking he's been let off easy until the third quarter, then unleash what I know you've got."

Nerves flooded his body once more and he hopped on the spot, rolled his shoulders out, and cracked his neck while listening to Coach address the rest of the team. The next thing he knew, they were jogging up the race into the brilliant sunshine and out onto the ground.

Dylan kept focus on Daniel as he led the team through their paces while allowing himself an occasional glance at the swelling stands of the city's sports ground. Thankfully, warm-up drills helped release the tension building up within him. Mum and Jack were somewhere out there. If only Dad could be here too.

"Right, guys. Huddle," Daniel said. "You heard Coach. Let's start the season by instilling fear in all who are watching. We have come to play and play hard. That premiership cup is ours. Stay hungry, stay focused, watch each other's backs!"

Dylan lifted his voice with his teammates as they cheered their captain before following him through the banner the cheer squad held up. As they crashed through, the crepe paper shredded into confetti and littered the field they were about to do battle on. A smile curled on Dylan's face. This was real.

Dylan spotted Hance heading for the center, and increased his jog to a steady run to man up. Jason fell into stride beside him.

"You ready, pup?" Jason asked.

Dylan chuckled, not breaking stride. How long would it be before until the 'baby' suggestions dropped off? It wasn't offensive, not coming from Jason. Instead, it felt brotherly. "You bet."

"Good. I watched you play a few games last year when I knew the club were interested in you." Jason spoke easily through their run. "I know what you can do, so let's give these guys a pair of Condors to talk about at their meeting tomorrow."

Dropping his head, Dylan exhaled a laugh. Unbelievable. He still couldn't believe they'd been watching him and he'd had no idea. He thanked God for the opportunity before him and asked for protection over him and his new team. As they approached the center and slowed their pace to a fast walk, Jason held his fist out across his chest. Dylan bumped it with his own. "Let's get 'em."

# TWENTY-EIGHT

"Walsh! Saunders!"

Coach Carter's voice boomed throughout the clubrooms, and Dylan's head jerked up. He watched his new Coach stride into the rooms from the post-match interviews, from his I'm-so-tired-anything-would-be-comfortable position on the floor. Were they in trouble? Dylan gave Jason a quick glance, but caught the beaming grin on his teammates face as Jason pushed himself to his feet, then reached a hand down to him. Dylan grasped it in a monkey grip and was jerked to his feet so fast his head spun.

He steadied himself as Coach Carter stopped before them and planted his fists on his hips. His face, tanned and deeply lined, was serious as he looked between the two of them. Dylan swallowed.

"You. Boys. Were. Sensational!" Coach's face dissolved into a broad smile as he thrust his arms into the air.

Beside him, Jason laughed, and their teammates applauded around them. Dylan looked around the room, lurching forward under a barrage of back slapping until the two firm hands of his Coach held his shoulders. He was chuckling.

"Look at him. He can't believe it! Someone give the boy a drink."

The game had gone by in a blur. Everything within Dylan's body felt good. He felt strong. He'd run easy, won contests, and surprised himself at how easily he shut down his opponent. He even managed to block out the crowd for most of the game. Only when the final siren blasted and the Condor's anthem boomed over the stadium did the roar of the crowd snap him back to where he was.

A crowd at a Valley Tigers game were never this loud. Or this big.

Dylan let his held breath out on a laugh and felt his body relax as he was jostled and praised by his coach and teammates. Their reaction had stunned him, but he knew they'd all worked together as a team.

"All right, all right!" He shouted, then laughed at the boys celebrating around him. "Jace and I weren't the only ones out on that field! Go Condors!"

Pumping the air with his fists, Dylan roared with his teammates until he was out of breath. The room was electrified. News reporters hurried around, clicking cameras filled the room with flashes, and laughter mingled with conversations rose to deafening pitch. A heavy arm fell across his shoulders and Dylan felt himself being moved from the hubbub towards the change rooms.

"They can't follow us in here!" Adam shouted in his ear. "You'll get used to them—the reporters, I mean."

Dylan sat back against his locker, thankful for the quiet cool of the change rooms. He closed his eyes and rested his head against the cool metal and breathed deeply. The sound of running water from the showers soothed his ringing ears. "That was intense."

"What?" Adam said beside him, "The game or the after-match celebrations?"

"Both." Dylan opened an eye to look at Adam before closing it again.

Somewhere in the room he heard Daniel chuckle. "You played well today, kid. Keep that up, and it's going to get a whole lot more intense for you."

"Hance didn't intimidate you at all, did he?"

Dylan opened his eyes and looked over at Dale. He shook his head. "No. Why would he have?"

Dale guffawed as he swung his towel over his shoulder. "You're nuts."

"Modesty isn't a strong card for you, is it?" Adam flipped his towel at Dylan before he left the room for the showers.

Dylan smirked and rolled his eyes. "That's not what I meant. I've watched him play for years, and Coach gave me good tips to play on him before we went out. You all looked after me out there, and I felt comfortable." He rose, turned towards his locker, opened it, and pulled his shower gear out. "Is that a bad thing? Do most new recruits roll over early on their first game or something?"

"We're just stirring," Daniel said from across the room. "You bite easy."

The quiet of the room erupted as more players entered from the clubrooms. They closed the door behind them, almost falling over themselves as they headed to their lockers, and the room settled into quiet once more. Dylan smiled as he made his way to the showers. This was his norm now. This was his career, and these boys would become closer than family. He shook his head in disbelief.

"Thank you, God." He murmured as he turned the shower on and relaxed under the pressure of the warm water over his weary body.

# TWENTY-NINE

"Since when do you bench press 136 kilos?"

A grin curled on Dylan's face as he rested the bar across his chest, focused once more, and pushed it up as Trent followed his movements. "The club's been working me up. They want me bench pressing over one-forty by June."

Trent's eyebrows raised, but he didn't comment.

Dylan knew his training schedule was bringing fast results. Coach said they needed him up to speed not only to sculpt him for appearance, but to give him the bulk he'd need in the area he'd be playing. While it was hard going, he did feel good by the results he was seeing, and the speed on ground he now had. Changing his diet was the hardest. No more visits to Hook & Cook, or he'd be in trouble with the dietitian.

A door opened and closed in the quiet men's workout room of The Valley Gymnasium Though neither Trent nor he took their eyes off the bar, Dylan knew they both knew it was Nick.

"Hey, man," Trent said.

"Fellas." Nick's voice echoed around the room.

"Ten more reps." Dylan's voice was strained as he held the bar up.

An exercise bike geared up as Nick started his circuit. One thing Dylan was happy about was that Sunday evenings were considered free time for the players, so he was able to continue his workouts at the local gym with his mates. Once he'd counted out ten more reps, he allowed Trent to take the bar out of his hands and he hung his arms loosely off his chest. "How's the LT going?" He asked, catching his breath.

"Not too bad." Trent said. "We are keeping the bases covered. Dave is a bit more hands-on now, but he says he's enjoying it."

"Your presence is missed though big fella." Nick said in between puffs. "The youth are sad you're not coming anymore, but always comment when they've seen you in the paper or when they've talked about you on the football shows."

Dylan chuckled as he sat up. "I caught one of those shows the other night. Honestly guys, it's embarrassing."

Nick grinned at him, his face beetroot red from exertion. "Has it sunk in yet?"

"No." Dylan grinned back at his friend.

"Been recognized in the street yet?" Trent asked, as he settled himself on the pec deck.

Dylan rose and crossed the room to the power tower. "It's only pre-season, guys."

"What do you say Trent," Nick puffed. "Give it one more week?"

"One more week." Trent grunted as he drew the pads together in front of his chest. "Or its your shout Nick next time we catch up at Beachside?"

Nick puffed while he considered Trent's offer. "Deal."

* * *

Eager to get as much out of his free time as he could, as soon as Dylan got home, he strode to the shed and pulled out the ride-on mower. The place was beginning to look unkempt. Mum hadn't said anything, but he knew it would be bothering her, and pigs would fly before Jack lifted a finger.

Resentment tried to rise up within him at the thought of Jack's laziness, but he squashed it easily. After the dramatic turn his life had taken, it was nice to keep some things normal—like gym with the boys and mowing the lawn. Plus, mowing the lawn was his time alone with God. Nobody could interrupt him. It was just him, his thoughts, and the land around him to tidy up. Not to mention the look on his Mum's face when she saw the lawn was mowed. It all added to his willingness to do the job.

An hour later, Dylan was rounding the house for the last time when a car coming up the driveway caught his attention, and triggered a memory. As he continued around the house to finish the edges, he tried to think why that car was familiar to him. He pushed the thought from his mind as he approached the gnome village Mum had set up at the rear of the house. He'd be a dead man if he wrecked her village.

Once he'd finished and all gnomes were accounted for, he drove the mower back to the shed. As the driveway came back into view, he saw the visiting car reversing back down the drive and Jack walking to the house. He frowned. He killed the mower's engine and pulled the earmuffs off. "Jack!" He called across the lawn. "All ok?"

"Yep. All good," Jack called back.

The backpack he carried seemed heavy for his slight frame. Dylan watched as he climbed the verandah steps, readjusted his backpack, stepped inside the house, and closed the front door.

Weird. What friend would stop in the middle of the driveway and reverse out? Dylan shook his head as he started the mower and drove it back to the shed. There was more to it.

"Hey Jack!" Dylan called, closing the front door behind him and pausing in the hallway. He couldn't hear the TV, so he stepped past the lounge room and entered the kitchen.

"What's up, bro?" Jack asked around a mouthful of food.

Dylan looked at the plate of an entire roast chicken Jack had in front of him, and shut the open fridge door. "Got enough food there?" He asked, a frown flickering over his brow as he pulled a seat up at the table. "I'm not paying extra board around here just so you can burn up more power either." Jack threw a scowl in Dylan's direction and picked at the chicken. Dylan shook his head. He cleared his throat. "You know, mum probably had that chicken earmarked for tea tonight."

"So." Jack took a large mouthful of a drumstick. "She can make something else."

Dylan felt his mouth press into thin line. He would not bite. He needed to get his brother to talk to him so he could work out what he was into.

"Who was in the car who couldn't be bothered dropping you off at the front door?"

Jack examined a piece of chicken before putting it in mouth. "Just a friend from uni."

"And they couldn't drop you at the front door?"

"Does it really matter what me and my friends do?"

The chicken smelled so good, Dylan felt his mouth watering. However, his new diet only allowed boiled chicken, not roasted. Would they really know if he had a piece though? Blinking, he squashed the temptation and pushed himself back from the table and crossed his arms. "It's just a bit odd. That's all."

"Yeah, well, I think your friends are odd too." Jack got up from the table, and crossed the floor to the pantry, pulled out a bottle of mustard and sweet chili sauce, then returned to the table.

"How is uni going?" Dylan asked, searching for common ground as Jack tipped the sauces over the chicken.

Jack glanced up at him. "It's good. Anymore questions?"

"You could speak in longer sentences."

"Maybe I just want to eat in peace. Can't you bother me another time?"

Dylan felt his jaw clench, and he pulled the plate away from Jack. "Excuse me?"

Jack was out of his seat quicker than Dylan had ever seen him move. He reached for the plate, but Dylan held it away from him.

"Gimme it back!" Jack spat at him.

"No. Not until you show some respect. What is your problem anyway?" Dylan looked up at Jack as if he had sprouted horns.

Jack rolled his eyes and crossed his arms in an exaggerated move. "Oh, well, let's see. I just get home and I just want –"

"Quit the attitude, Jack." Dylan rose to his feet and put the chicken back in the fridge. "You forget who you speak too far too often around here."

When he turned back to face Jack, he noticed a slight tremor in his arms. He radiated scarcely controlled anger. Dylan raised an eyebrow. There was nothing Jack could do, and he knew it. He waited to see if Jack would apologize, but he shoved his chair out of the way and stormed from the room. A piece of paper floated to the floor from his back pocket as he went.

The paper jogged a memory: the paper, the car, the late-night visit. He lunged for the paper as Jack reappeared, his demeanor strangely calm as he held a hand out, his unblinking gaze on the paper in Dylan's hand. "Can I have that back. Please."

"This?" Dylan asked, his tone nonchalant as he held the paper up for Jack to see, but out of his reach. "Why? What's on it you don't want me to see?"

"Nothing."

"So you won't mind if I have a look then?" Dylan began to open the folded paper.

Jack stepped forward. "No!"

"So someone driving the same car as the one I saw not even an hour ago, gives it to you in the middle of the night, and won't drop you at the front door. You're standing there like your life hangs in the balance, and you say it's nothing?"

Jack's mouth dropped open and something flickered in his eyes moments before Dylan found himself thrust back into the fridge door.

Before Dylan could react, a second shove saw magnets and overdue bills spill from behind Dylan and drove the air from his lungs. Jack grabbed and clawed at him, tearing Dylan's shirt from his body. Jack's strength was overwhelming, but Dylan kept his grasp on the paper while trying to wrestle Jack away from him. He grabbed both Jack's wrists in one hand and moved to free himself from the corner, when one more thrust from Jack caused him to overbalance and slip on the papers over the floor. Dylan hit the kitchen floor hard. Jack landed on top of him, intensifying his desperate attempt to get the paper and Dylan felt the chain of his dog tag break. Anger burst inside him.

"What is going on in here?" Mum shrieked from the doorway.

Dylan used the distraction to shove Jack away. Jack stumbled to his feet, searched the floor, scooped up the ripped pieces of paper, and dashed from the room.

# THIRTY

"Leave him." Mum held a hand up to Dylan.

Dylan slumped back onto his elbows, and looked over at Mum, his expression fierce. "Leave him? Look at me!" Mum leaned against the kitchen bench, chewing a fingernail while staring at the mess on the floor. She looked every bit of her fifty-one years of age yet as vulnerable as a small child, and Dylan's anger dissipated fast. He'd never seen Mum so defeated.

"Now do you believe me? I told you he could be like this months ago," Mum said, her voice shaky as it broke into the silence of the room. When she shifted her gaze to him, Dylan shook his head and bundled all the papers over the floor up, snatched up his broken chain and tag and rose to his feet. He placed the papers on the table. "What are these?"

Mum looked away. Dylan splayed the papers out over the table to take a better look at them. They were bills. All bills. "Mum, I said I could help out with the bills. You don't need to—"

"I don't need any help from you. You're the child here."

Dylan could see Mum was on shaky ground. He took a deep breath and kept his voice calm. "I know, but it wouldn't be a problem."

Mum closed her eyes and crossed her arms. Dylan knew her look all too well: she'd shut down and the conversation was over. He sighed. "I'm going to check Jack's room."

With a prayer for calm, Dylan strode down the hall to Jack's room, pushed open the door, and stood at the threshold taking in the sight before him. He couldn't see the floor. He could see a disheveled bed, with food wrappers, and empty booze bottles littering the bedside tables. Open drawers on his tallboy spilling their contents on top of the mess on the floor, while the wardrobe doors sat ajar, unable to be closed.

The silence was pierced by his ringing phone. He ripped the phone from his back pocket, but didn't recognize the number calling him.

"Dylan speaking." He stepped gingerly into his brother's room, dubious about where to put each foot. No one spoke from the other end of the phone.

"Hello?" He barked down the line, unable to keep the annoyance from his voice. He caught sight of a piece of paper sticking out from under the bed and moved towards it. Slowly, carefully.

"Jack's staying with me for a few days," a young-sounding female voice said.

He pulled up short as the hair on the back of his neck rose. "Who is this?"

"You don't know me," the voice said. "Oh, and Jack said to stay out of his room."

The line went dead. Dylan checked his call log and found the number at the top of the received calls list. He smirked. "Not smart enough to block your number, I see."

Jack had been trouble for a while, and Dylan finally felt he might find out why. He pulled the paper out from under the bed.

It was an empty window envelope, with no writing or postmarks. Useless. He dropped the envelope to the floor. What was going on with Jack? Moody, disorganized, strange friends, scoffs food, late nights, surprising strength ... he could read the signposts but didn't want to believe what they said. Not drugs. Not his brother.

With one last look around the room, Dylan stepped back into the hallway and shut the door behind him. He knew one thing: if Jack had slipped up once, he'll slip up again.

\* \* \*

Dylan lifted his glass with the other boys at his table, cheering the end of their three game pre-season campaign. Even though they had lost this last game, Dylan had had the time of his life. And the premiership season hadn't even begun.

The marquee erected on the riverbank was elaborately decorated with chiffon curtains and fairy lights. A live band played to a full dance floor and waiters in penguin suits floated around each table. The city lights sparkled in the inky blackness of the water, while distant laughter from the botanical gardens floated on the breeze. He could scarcely believe he was here. Such a beautiful mild evening, spent in celebration. This was living.

"A toast!" Tom declared, refilling his glass. "To our illustrious new recruit. Number twenty-seven, Dylan Saunders."

Surprised, Dylan met Tom's eyes over the table as he lifted his glass with everyone else. They hadn't much to do with each other. They played opposite ends of the field and had barely spoke two words to each other since they'd declared a truce. Why was Tom raising a toast to him?

Tom drained his glass while keeping his gaze steady. Dylan lowered his glass without taking a sip. "Thanks, Tom. I appreciate it."

"Enjoy your night. You deserve it."

Tom raised his glass once more, then stood and meandered towards another table while the boys began speaking in hushed tones.

"Tom's full as a boot already."

"He's got something planned."

Laughter.

"Hasn't he always? Look at him…moving towards the dance floor now."

More laughter.

Dylan felt an elbow in his side, and he turned his gaze from the dance floor to Dale, misgivings about Tom swirling inside him.

"Don't worry about the toast." Dale said. "He usually toasts the newbies. He acts tough, but he's mush underneath."

"Thanks, mate."

A new voice entered the conversation at their table. A female voice. Dylan turned to see who had joined them.

She was young. He guessed nineteen, maybe twenty years old. From her flushed cheeks and revealing dress, he suspected she would be a regular at these functions, a regular with one thing in mind. She turned and caught his eye, and her eyes widened notably.

"Hi! I'm Sarah," she said, her voice breathy. "Are you having a fun night?"

Dylan acknowledged her greeting and tried to think of a polite way to excuse himself, uncomfortable beneath her intense gaze and the suggestive way she moved to the music.

"You've had a great start to the year. I read you were recruited from The Valley Tigers. How are you settling in with the Condors?"

Dylan caught Jason's eye from across the room and sent a mental plea for help, then flicked his gaze back to Sarah. "It's been great. The boys have been very supportive."

"It's a great team. I've been a Condor since I was ten years old, but only got my membership two years ago, when I turned eighteen."

Dylan made a mental note. Twenty years old. "Well, it's good to meet a dedicated supporter."

She laughed and stepped closer. Dylan looked for escape as he felt an arm fall across his shoulders. Jason. Thank goodness.

"Excuse me, darlin'. I need the big fella for a moment."

Before he knew it, Dylan was seated at Jason's table. "You better get used to this. The more well-known you become, the more the girls will be all over you."

"As they are with you." Daniel lazed back in his chair and drummed his butter knife on the white table cloth. He looked bored. Dylan glanced at Jason, who didn't reply. Instead, he reached for his drink with a lopsided grin formed on his face.

"Hey, fellas. Check out the tribute to evolution at ten o'clock." Tom appeared at the table. As everyone began casting not-so-subtle glances towards the bar, Tom slapped Dylan on the shoulder. "I suppose I should say she's a fine creation. Right, Saunders?"

Alcohol-induced laughter broke out at their table as Dylan glanced at Tom. Tom was looking for a bite with such a comment, but Dylan wouldn't debate God's word with a drunk man. Instead, he rose as catcalls and comments were made, and headed back to his own table with a smile.

The conversation at his own table was similar. What the girls were wearing, who was an easy pick up, what parties they'd been to, what funny experiences they'd had. Dylan half listened while the band played. Their laughter began to grate on him. He felt the absence of his friends like a widening chasm, and he missed the fun, wholesome, and meaningful nature of their conversations.

# THIRTY-ONE

Dylan's stomach rolled and he took a sip of water. Nerves. He thought the three pre-season games would have settled the horrible feeling of anxiety before a game, but he hardly slept a wink last night, and he'd been up before the birds to go for a run.

Now, pacing the hallway of the family home, he didn't feel any better. Should he eat something? Or would that make him throw up? He paused between the lounge room and kitchen: sit down, or go eat?

The house phone rang, and Dylan strode into the lounge and snatched it out of its cradle. "Hello. Dylan speaking."

"Dylan Saunders?"

Dylan leaned against the fireplace mantle, looked out the window at the horses feeding in the nearby paddocks. "Yeah, this is Dylan. Who's speaking?"

"AFL Dylan?" The male voice said, his tone testing. "Big day for you, isn't it?"

Straightening as if an icy finger ran up his spine, Dylan gripped the phone. "Who is this?"

"Bet you make a bit of money now …"

Silence held Dylan's tongue. A calm he didn't understand cleared his mind and he waited the caller out. The guy wouldn't answer any questions he asked anyway …

"That's handy."

The line went dead. Dylan was playing over the unspoken threat when movement to his left drew his attention to Jack shuffling into the kitchen. He narrowed his eyes as Jack pulled the puffed rice cereal from the cupboard then sat heavily at the table. Jack was up to no good, and the phone call was just one more hint. However, if he confronted Jack, his brother would probably deny everything then disappear again. They hadn't spoken two words to each other since Jack had returned, but Dylan had heard him talking to Mum—somewhat respectfully for once.

Jack looked over at him, as if sensing he was being watched. Dylan held his gaze, daring him to look away first. He needed to talk to Nick, but he needed more to go on first.

And he had a game to play.

When Jack looked back to the bowl of cereal in front of him, Dylan scooped up his sports bag and left the house. He would deal with Jack later.

Just under an hour later, Dylan parked his bike in the underground players' parking area of the Condor's ground, and made his way inside. Two hours until first bounce. The nerves were starting to make themselves known again and he couldn't let them overtake him. He would play today as he'd played in the pre-season games: all in.

Daniel met him as he entered the change rooms and dumped his bag in his locker. "Dylan, how are you feeling?"

"I'm ready to go." Well, he would be if his pulse would slow down and breathing got easier. Was it nerves, or was something else rattling his cage this morning? A frown tickled his brow as he stretched his quads. Daniel clapped a hand on his shoulder. "You're nervous. It's normal. First big game. Sellout crowd. Trust me, those nerves will disappear the moment you jog out onto the ground."

Dylan took a breath through his mouth. "Thanks, Daniel. Not sure why I'm so keyed up this morning. Just can't wait to get out there."

Daniel offered a few tips to help Dylan play his man. As Dylan listened, his mind settled on the job he had been given to do. He knew the player Coach Carter had manned him up with. Garth Fraser was aggressive and played hard. What he lacked in size, he made up for it in strength. Dylan could recall a number of times he'd seen players injured while playing on him, and he asked God to protect him—and protect Jack, and their home.

"All right boys!" Adam said, bursting into the change rooms. "Are we ready?"

All around him, Dylan's teammates shouted their readiness in response. Their voices filled the room as they punched their fists into the air and scruffed one another. Dylan laughed, relaxing. The nerves tightening his chest had finally let up. With a shout, he joined in the boisterous fun of boosting each other up until Coach Carter entered the rooms to give the last-minute pep talk.

Dylan fell into line as the team began to file out onto the ground, fired up and itching to get on the ground. The crowd erupted as the first of his team spilled out over the run, and his blood ran hot. As their banner came into view, he couldn't help but smile. Game on!

Four quarters later, Dylan stood in the middle of his team as their club song rang out. He linked his hands behind his head as he slowly took in the exiting crowd, the cheer squads waving banners, and his teammates hugging and high fiving each other.

If only this feeling could last forever. "Dylan!" Daniel pounded him on the back. "What a weapon you are! Well done, boy."

Before he could thank Daniel, Dale and Jason joined them and grabbed him in a bear hug, roughly manhandling him while laughing and hooting against his ear until he ordered them to put him down.

"That mark you took was a screamer!" Dale said. "The way you came down from it I was sure you'd have broken your collarbone."

Dylan shook his head. "I'm fine, mate. No damage done."

"Beginner's luck," Daniel said, shepherding them to start walking from the ground as news reporters and cameramen, began heading towards them. "You be careful, Saunders. Marks like that from a big man like yourself can end in serious injuries."

"I've taken many, and I'm fine," Jason said, giving his captain a playful shove.

"Mr. Saunders," a reporter said, hurrying towards them. "A moment of your time?"

Dylan glanced at his captain, who gave him a "go-for-it" gesture. He halted on the ground while his teammates continued towards the clubrooms. As Dylan looked back at the reporter, he took a quick step back. The cameraman was a little too close for his liking.

"There's certainly a lot of talk about you, the new and exciting recruit for the Condors. How are you feeling about the year ahead?"

Cameras flashed and he heard his name called from the boundary line as the reporter waited patiently in front of him. Dylan ran a hand over his hair. "Ah, I'm feeling positive. The boys have been very supportive and we're looking forward to what the year ahead brings."

"And so are we. The mark you took in the third quarter certainly had everyone out of their seats. Can we expect more of that from you each week?"

Dylan chuckled. He dropped his gaze and rubbed the back of his neck. He'd never had so much interest in how he played football before. He'd taken many marks off his opponent's backs while playing for the Tigers, and no one paid much attention apart from a cheer or two in the clubrooms afterwards. "Yeah, I think so." He glanced back to the Condor's race as the last of his teammates disappeared from view. "I'm just going to bring my best game each week, and we'll see what happens."

"Thank you for your time," the reporter said, and gestured to her cameraman to lower the camera.

"Thanks." Dylan turned towards the run and sprinted to catch up with his teammates.

He soon broke through the crowds in the clubrooms and stepped into the cool quiet of the change room. His phone rang from inside his locker.

"Your phone's been ringing for the last five minutes," Adam said, rubbing his hair down with a towel. "Some girl sweet on you after seeing you on TV?"

"They all become interested after you're recognizable." Dale muttered.

"Dale, get over her!" Tom flicked his locker closed and hefted his bag over his shoulder. "She wasn't that good anyway."

"Listen—Daniel placed a hand on Dale's shoulder. "How about Dylan answer that damn phone, and you and Tom stop arguing over Tanya. We're all sick of that saga."

Dylan tried to hide his grin as he unlocked his locker and pulled out his bag to fish out his phone. At times, joining this club felt like he'd tuned into a daytime soapy that had been running for years.

He grabbed his phone. Nine missed calls and five messages. All from Mum. Alarm set his heart racing as he opened one of the messages:

*'We've been burgled! Call me back ASAP!'*

# THIRTY-TWO

Dylan grabbed the handrail and propelled himself up the veranda steps and into his family home.

"Mum! You here?" A chair scrapped the wooden floor, and Mum appeared in the doorway of the kitchen. He gave her a long hug before releasing her and stepping back. "Are you ok? What happened?"

She took a shaky breath, made her way back into the kitchen, and she sat before looking back up at him. "I called the police, but there's nothing they can do."

"What was taken?" Dylan looked out of the kitchen into the upturned lounge room.

"I don't think anything has been taken, but the police said they seemed to be looking for something." Mum's voice sounded empty and distant. "They asked me all these questions about

Jack and other people, people I don't know and places I've never heard off."

Dylan sat at the table. The question he dreaded to ask burned on his tongue. "Did they ask you anything about … about drugs?"

Mum lifted her head sharply, her expression incredulous. "You don't think Jacky is on drugs, do you?"

"I don't want to think it, but I can't help it." Dylan stood, restless and not wanting to go through the reasons for his suspicion. "I'm going to check my room and the rest of the house."

What would his room look like? Dylan glanced at Jack's closed bedroom door. There was no point checking Jack's room for signs of disturbance. It was already a mess, and he'd never know even if someone had been in there.

Dylan pushed open his door. As suspected, it had been rummaged through—overturned bed with sheets stripped off, drawers pulled out, TV turned over, and the contents of his wardrobe were spilled over the floor. He couldn't see anything missing. Whoever had been in here was looking for something in particular, probably money.

He had to talk to Nick.

"I'm going to see Nick." Dylan strode back up the hallway, passing Mum in the kitchen. "I'll be back in an hour or so."

Within ten minutes Dylan pulled his bike into Nick's driveway. Nick's Clubsport was in the driveway as were both his sisters' cars. The neighborhood was quiet, and Dylan could almost hear the gentle crash of waves along Main Beach, just one block away.

Adrenaline from the game and learning their home had been ransacked was wearing down, and a deep tiredness began to seep into his limbs. He pulled his helmet off, praying for strength, as Nick stepped out of the house and strolled towards him.

"Hey, brother, what brings you around? Didn't you just wrap a game up less than two hours ago?"

"I did." Dylan remained seated on his bike. His legs felt like concrete. "Look, I think we have serious trouble with Jack on our hands. Our house was hit while I was playing and Mum was at the shops."

Nick's face transformed before his eyes. His eyes turned to steel as his stance widened and he crossed his arms. "Go on."

Dylan filled Nick in on the car he'd seen around their home, the fight over a piece of paper, and the surprising strength Jack had at times. "Drugs is all I can conclude. What do you think?"

"We need more to go on," Nick said. "Keep an eye on his behavior. Note down when he goes out and when he comes home. Try to get the number plate of the car. And we'll need any other clues or information you can get."

"What about phone numbers?" He pulled out his phone and scrolled to the record of the anonymous call. "I have this."

After telling Nick the story behind the number, he read the digits out to Nick to record on his notepad.

"I'll run this tomorrow and see what comes up. In the meantime, act dumb. Don't let on you suspect anything. And please try to get your mum to keep her mouth shut."

"I'll do my best." Mum was prone to a bit of gossip, and she'd been worse since Dad died when she developed PTSD. She was almost unstoppable with her need to talk to people. About everything! "I'll try to get her to understand she has to keep quiet, but I can't guarantee she'll remain that way for long. Something will slip out."

Nick linked his hands behind his head and sighed. "Maybe suggest someone she can talk to if she needs to. Someone like Lexi. They get along well."

"Good idea," Dylan slipped his phone back into the bike's saddle bag. "I better get going. See what I can clean up before Jack gets home."

"Before you go, we have a youth social next Saturday night. We're having a drive-in movie night at the church grounds. If it's not a game night, we'd love to see you."

Dylan started the bike, eager to get going, and its roar echoed around the beachside neighborhood.

Nick dipped his head. "Understood."

Dylan pulled out of Nick's place, his mind abuzz with haphazard thoughts. He had to get home and clean the place up before Jack got home. He had to have a conversation with Mum about her need for gossip and try to redirect her. He had to find time to observe his brother somewhere in his crazy schedule. How was he meant to do that? Where would he find the time?

At least he had a close friend who was a cop. That was something to be thankful for.

Cruising through the main street of The Valley, scents coming from Hook & Cook filled his nostrils and his stomach cramped. He hadn't enjoyed his favorite fast food since he he'd signed with the Condors. As a team they were told not eat fast food in no uncertain terms. Main Street's traffic lights turned red. Dylan pulled his bike up, his gaze drawn to the flashing light bulbs outside Hook & Cook. Who would know if he took some food home?

His mouth began to water.

The lights turned green, and Dylan pulled into the first available car park.

After the day he'd had, he needed some greasies. If anyone asked, he was taking food home for his family.

# THIRTY-THREE

The evening was calm and illuminated in shades of cool blue from the full moon above. Dylan pulled his bike up at the church grounds and kicked out the foot stand, his stomach fluttering as he removed his bike gear. Lexi would be here tonight, and he was looking forward to seeing her again. He hadn't told her he was coming, and he was anticipating her expression when she saw him.

With a quick look over the packed car park, Dylan made his way towards the back of the church grounds to where Nick had told him the movie screen was going to be set up.

The sight that greeted him was amazing. Lexi must have done the decorating. Food and coffee vans lined the back fence, fairy lights and balloons crisscrossed over the seating area, and soft music played in the background. It all combined to create a warm and inviting place. Lexi's style.

"Dylan, Dylan, Dylan!"

A smiled turned up the corners of Dylan's face as some of the youth ran towards him, darting in and around the people seated on the grass. They were breathless when they gathered around him, panting and pulling at his arms. "We saw you on TV!"

"What's it like, playing AFL?"

"Were you hurt in that tackle last week?"

"We haven't seen you for ages."

The questions came fast, drawing a laugh from him. He took in their bright eyes and eager expressions and was about to start answering, but the last comment made his answers catch in his mouth. His smile dimmed a little. He knew Matt wasn't accusing him but stating a fact: they hadn't seen him in ages because he hadn't been in ages.

Regret sat heavily within him, and he sighed. "I know, buddy. I'll try to be here more often from now on."

The young people took his word with bright smiles and nodding heads.

"Dylan!" He glanced over his shoulder, he caught Hope waving at him. He waved back before looking back at the youth. "Guys, I better grab a seat, but how about we have a bit of a kick-to-kick after the movies finish tonight?"

The looks of sheer excitement that flashed over their faces before they darted back to their picnic rugs filled Dylan with peace over his absence. Kids were so understanding.

With hellos and hurried conversations, Dylan picked his way across the lawn to where Hope was seated. It was great to see the friendly faces of his church family again, and he couldn't wipe the smile off his face as he sat down. "Hey Hope, how's it going?"

"I'm fabulous!" She answered with a toss of her shaggy bob. "It's good to see you, stranger. Where have you been?"

Dylan laid down on the rug, propped himself up on his elbows and crossed his ankles. "I've been fairly busy, and Jack's been a handful."

Hope nodded her head and shifted herself to sit cross-legged. "Sorry to hear that. I wish he'd come back to youth. Maybe it'd help him."

Dylan changed the subject, not wanting to talk about Jack. "So where's Josh? Will he be joining us later?"

"Nope." Hope fished through her picnic basket and pulled out a bag of chips. "I'm flying solo."

A brown bag landed in his lap. He jumped, looking up in time to see Nick drop another bag in his lap.

"Good to see you. Hot dog with sauce, and popcorn for later."

"Thanks, Nick." Dylan settled onto his side while biting hungrily into the hot dog. Nick didn't know about the no-fast-food rule at the club, and Dylan wasn't about to tell him.

"Here we go. Drinks for everyone."

The sound of Lexi's voice brought Dylan's head up sharply, and she glanced at him. Her eyes widened as her face boomed with color.

"Hey, you! I'm sorry I didn't know you were coming."

Dylan finished his mouthful through a closed smile, enjoying her blush. "Surprise."

"I'll grab you a drink." Lexi put down the drinks she was carrying. "What would you like?"

"Have a seat, Lexi," Trent said gently. "I'll duck back over and grab the man a drink."

Dylan chuckled and held up his sports drink. "Guys, it's ok. I've got a drink."

"What's it like playing big league footballer now?" Lexi asked, relaxing as she retook her seat and turned up collar of her coat.

Dylan swirled the liquid in his bottle as he thought how to answer. He was having the time of his life, but he didn't want to sound ungrateful for the unforgettable times he'd had with them at youth group. "It's ... intense. Hard going during the week, but the adrenaline rush after the game is incredible."

The smile that lit Lexi's face told him she was happy for him, and he smiled back at her, wanting to ask how she had been, when Hope tapped his arm. "Shh. The movie is about to start. We can discuss football and how buff you've become after the movie's finished."

As the lights above them dimmed, Dylan turned to the big screen to watch the previews, ignoring Hope's last comment. A weight pressed against his legs, he dropped his eyes from the screen to see the back of Hope's head. Uncomfortable, he flicked a glance at his friends but they were all watching the movie. He'd wait until intermission to reposition himself, so not to draw attention.

It was distracting. Every time Hope laughed, or commented to Lexi over the rug about the movie, she inched further up his legs. By intermission, she was almost leaning back against his chest. When the movie finished and the lights were turned up, he got some odd glances from his friends. Announcements came over the PA system. The food and drink vans were still open, there were games for the kids to play, and a car had left their lights on. Hope pushed herself up. "How great was that movie?" she asked.

"Yeah, I love it," Lexi said. Her voice notably flat and Dylan caught the quick glance she threw in his direction.

"The next one is even better. Pastor Walker let me pick it." Hope turned to Dylan and gave him a playful punch in the arm. "You better stay awake for it."

"I'm doing my best." Dylan ignored the warning that flashed through his mind at her smile.

Beside him, Lexi rose and smoothed out her skirt. "Hope, I need a cuppa, or I might doze off during the next one. Come for a walk?"

Hope picked at one of her fingernails, her face tilted up at Lexi as if she'd been asked what the square root of pi was. While she was distracted, Dylan used the opportunity to move away from Hope. Once he was standing, Hope rose and Lexi looped her arm, guiding her through the people towards the food vans.

Nick cleared his throat and Dylan looked over at him while stretching out his shoulders.

"Something you want to tell us?" Nick asked, eyebrows raised.

Dylan shook his head as he sat down on the picnic rug once more. "No!"

"So there's nothing going on between you and Hope, yet she leans against you while watching a movie? In public?"

"I don't know what that was all about, but she was very casual when I asked about Josh." Dylan took a quick look over his shoulder to make sure the girls were out of hearing. "How are things with them? They're still on, right?"

Trent shrugged. "They're going through a rough patch. That's all we know."

"They're coming." Nick said, and lay down on the picnic rug again, his eyes upward towards the screen.

Dylan pulled his legs in to sit cross-legged, figuring Hope wouldn't be so bold as to try and lean against him while he was sitting up, and took a long drink from his bottle.

As long as Lexi didn't think there was anything going on with Hope. That was all he cared about.

# THIRTY-FOUR

*D*ylan roughly dried his hair then threw the bath towel over the shower. He'd risen early and decided to and go watch The Valley Tigers play. Maybe he could talk to Josh after the game. He was still bothered by Hope's behavior last night.

Dylan rubbed the stubble forming on his jaw wondering if he should shave or not. He turned to the mirror, aware of how much his chest and shoulders had filled out. A grin tipped his mouth as he looked over his abdominals to where they met his hip flexors. For the first time, he was thankful for the club's extreme diet. He would rope in the next pinch test.

Feeling good, Dylan decided not to shave. It felt good to not be perfectly groomed before he stepped out for once. He left the bathroom, dressed quickly, and hurried from the house, not wanting to get caught up discussing something with Mum or run into Jack. He just wanted to check in with Josh.

The Valley Tigers home ground was at full capacity. The Vipers team bus was pulled up behind the Tigers club house, which explained why: today's game was a grudge match. Keen to see how Josh captained the club against this long-standing rival, Dylan pulled his aviators down off his head and crossed the car park to the stands to watch the game.

It was a close match. The Tigers kept up for three quarters, but were going down in flames in the last quarter. Dylan made his way to the fence by the Tigers interchange bench and peered around the shelter looking for Coach Davis.

"Dylan!" Josh said, scooting over the bench seat towards him. "It is great to see you, mate"

Dylan shook his hand. "You too. Where's Coach Davis?"

Josh turned back to follow the game. One of the Vipers was lining up in front of goals. "He's sick. Our assistant coach is on the phone."

"What's happening to you boys? Have you run out of puff?" Dylan watched the Viper player thread the ball between the two goalposts.

Josh shook his head. "I have no idea. They've just lifted, and we can't catch them."

An old teammate jogged to the bench to change places with Josh.

"I'll catch up with you after the game, there is only ten minutes to go." Josh said as he ran out onto the field.

Disappointed to see his old team going down to their archrivals, Dylan retook his seat and counted down the minutes until the final siren rang out. Without a second look at the scoreboard, Dylan got up to make his way into the clubroom, but he found himself surrounded by young kids.

"See, I told you it was him!" One kid said, elbowing his friend before shoving a pad and pen up to Dylan. "Can you sign, can you sign?"

"Me first! I spotted him before you."

"Doesn't matter. I asked him first." The first child stepped closer.

Dylan retook his seat, chuckling at their insistence. Three more kids appeared, talking as fast as the first two.

Taking their pens and picture cards of himself to sign, he entertained their questions with good patience until their parents came over and shepherded the kids away. Finally free, Dylan made his way to the clubrooms to catch up with Josh.

He found Josh showered and relaxing at the bar, talking with the assistant coach. Dylan was stopped few times to talk to old teammates, but finally made it to the bar and pulled up a seat beside Josh.

After engaging in small talk with the assistant coach for a while, he finally left and Dylan was alone with Josh.

"I want to talk to you about Hope." Dylan poured himself another drink of water from the jug on the bar. "Is everything ok with you two?"

Josh cleared his throat. "I'm not too sure."

"What's been happening that makes you think you're on rocky ground?"

"She's just gone quiet on me." Josh ruffled his hair. "She can usually talk the leg off an iron pot, so when she's quiet you know there's something wrong."

Dylan frowned. "From what I hear, she's still attending church functions—"

"What are we talking about over here, kids?" Max leaned between them and grabbed the bowl of peanuts on the bar.

Dylan swallowed his annoyance. "How's it going, Max?"

Max shoveled mouthful after mouthful of peanuts in. "Fit as a mallee bull and twice as dangerous. How's the big time treating ya?"

Dylan answered Max's questions quickly, hoping he'd get the hint and leave so he and Josh could finish their conversation. If Max caught on, he didn't care. Instead, he turned to Josh. "How's that pretty little thing you're dating? Is she still on the scene?"

Josh's usual amiable expression changed as he eyeballed Max. Dylan was about to break the standoff when Josh took a sip of his drink. "Max, this conversation doesn't involve you. Leave us to it, thanks."

The grin on Max's face remained as bright as when he first burst in on them, and only brightened as he replaced the now-empty bowl on the counter. "Sure thing, Cap. Say hi to Hope for me."

Max sauntered off, and Josh threw the rest of his drink back.

"What was that about?" Dylan asked.

"Max is a known flirt. It's nothing."

"As long as it's nothing to Hope." Dylan finished his drink and placed it the empty glass on the counter. "She's been acting a little funny around me lately. I wanted to let you know."

"All I can gather is that there's some trouble on her home front. She's not talking much about it, but I haven't been to her place in months. She doesn't want me coming over."

Dylan frowned. "So are you two still on?"

"As far as I know."

"Ok. My advice is to keep Hope away from here until you two are sorted. By the sounds of things, the last thing she needs is Max having a crack at her."

# THIRTY-FIVE

Rain was forecast for the evening and the biting autumn wind suggested it wasn't far off. At least that was something Dylan knew for sure … unlike the afternoon which hadn't provided the answers he sought. Instead, it turned out to give him more questions.

Gearing down, Dylan turned into his long driveway and coasted towards the open shed. Rain tapped on his helmet and leathers, the gentle rhythm soothing his worry. The calming scents of gravel, cut hay, and sweet eucalyptus wove their way under his helmet and he breathed them in. If it wasn't for the wind chill, he'd sit on the porch, watch the rain, and try to make sense of what was happening.

Once he'd parked and locked his bike, Dylan made his way towards the house. A black BMW was parked under the mature peppercorn tree by the house. A weight developed in his gut at the sight of the strange car, and he quickened his pace. As he leapt onto the porch, he could hear raised voices inside. He ripped open the front door and strode into the lounge.

Two men in dark suits had his mum cornered by the fireplace. Her face was flushed, and her hands were shaking.

"I told you, I don't know where he is, so just leave."

"What's going on?" Dylan dumped his helmet and bike jacket on the couch, clearly surprising the two men. They turned to face him. "Mum? Who are these guys?"

"I don't know, but they won't leave!" Her voice broke, and her knuckles whitened on the mantel.

Dylan was head and shoulders taller than the men in the room, but they weren't the sort of men who would be phased by his size. They looked like the kind who could fight, and fight dirty if need be. He straightened.

"Who are you looking for?"

The dark-haired man slipped on a pair of sunglasses before answering. "Jack. Where is he?"

The blonde man slipped on a pair of sunglasses as well, and a tingle of warning zipped up Dylan's spine. He stepped closer, hoping his size might send a message to their unwanted guests.

"I have no idea." He lifted his shoulder indifferently, keeping his eyes on them. "Jack comes and goes as he pleases. Who are you? Can we take a message?"

The two men exchanged a glance. One nodded, and the other reached into his shirt. Mum shrieked and buried her face in the mantle. Dylan stepped forward as firm hand slapped him on the chest.

"Make sure Jack gets this." The dark-haired man said.

He removed his hand and turned to leave. A business card tumbled from where his hand had been. Dylan caught the card before it hit the floor, turning as the second man left the room. After they left, he shut the door firmly behind them, and dead-locked the door.

Dylan turned the card over in his hand and read the back but didn't recognize the name. A thump sounded from the lounge room. He ducked back into the lounge and found Mum slumped against the fireplace. "Mum! You all right?" He asked, coming to her side.

Her dilated eyes fixed on him as she grabbed his shirt. "Who were they? Is Jacky in trouble?"

Jack was more than in trouble if two goons were visiting their home at night, but as he embraced his Mum, he dismissed her concern. "Are you all right?" he asked again. She nodded weakly against him, and he rested his chin on her head. He had to talk to Nick again. He had to find out who those men were and where his brother was before the men found Jack … or came back.

* * *

"Saunders! You're up."

"How'd you go?" Dylan asked as Jason sat beside him. The monthly check-in to be weighed, measured, and have the pinch test done by the dietician wasn't something they looked forward to … well, most of them didn't. Tom often left the room smiling like he'd just won Lotto.

Jason slipped the cap off his head and shot Dylan a not-so-good glance. "Still can't budge that last bit of fat."

The door opened. "Saunders. Dylan Saunders?"

"You better go," Jason said. "I'll catch you afterwards."

Dylan entered Ren Hart's office feeling confident with the improvements he'd been making. One look at the man's serious face told him he was way off. Dylan took a seat, unsure of what to expect. Ren looked down to the file on the desk then back up at him.

"Dylan, I'm a little disappointed by a report I heard about you this month."

Dylan sat forward in his seat. "I'm sorry. What do you mean?"

"I have been informed you purchased a substantial amount of takeaway food a couple weeks back." Ren took a quick look the notes in front of him. "Fish and chips, to be specific."

The lie Dylan rehearsed while waiting for his greasies came to mind, and it almost flew out of his mouth but his conscience put a clamp on it. Stunned, he looked back at Ren. Ren shut the file in front of him and clasped his hands over it.

"You're not denying it. Good. But this does set you back in the program, so I've increased your cardio and weights, and I want to see you twice next week."

Even though he tried to listen to what Ren was saying, Dylan was lost in thought. How did Ren know he'd broke the strict diet program? Had someone ratted him out? If so, who?

"Send Walters in. Thanks."

Realizing he had been dismissed, Dylan stood and left the office. A chill ran over him as he re-entered the clubrooms and informed Sam Walters that he was next. How much did the club know about him? Or his family.

A firm slap on the back roused him from his zombie-like trance and the sound of Jason's chuckle entered his thoughts. He turned to his teammate and found him grinning ear to ear. "You look like you've been given bad news," Jason said. "Do you have to do extra cardio too?"

"And weights."

"Heard you were a bad boy." Jason leaned in to emphasis his point, his hazel eyes twinkling with delight. "They have eyes everywhere."

Dylan raised an eyebrow. "Yeah, I figured that." Turning towards the exit, he called over his shoulder. "Come on. We have laps to do."

# THIRTY-SIX

Game Day had come and Dylan wasn't ready.

Irritable and frustrated, he ran his hands over his hair and leaned back against his locker. The clubrooms were bustling, so Dylan had retreated to the change rooms for some much-needed quiet.

His mind wasn't focused and his concern wasn't about winning, but whatever was going on with Jack. He'd been praying all week for God to watch over Jack and make sure he was safe, for someone to jolt him back onto the right path, for something to happen to bring everything to light. Dylan's chest felt tight and he took a deep breath and yawned. The Bible said not to feel anxious about anything, but anxious was all he was feeling. All he'd been feeling for days.

"Let's go boys. Go get 'em!" Coach Carter shouted at the top of his voice. While his teammates responded with guttural roars, Dylan merely clapped his hands as he rejoined his team in the clubrooms. When the team ran out onto the grounds, Dylan jogged last in line. He'd never felt so distracted when running out onto the ground, a feeling which added to his list of prayers as he jogged—prayers for his own safety.

His opponent was a newish player to the league, and he hadn't had time to study him. Determined not to let his lack of homework show, Dylan resolved to throw himself into game and play like he was with the Tigers.

He never studied his opponents back then.

As the umpire bounced the first bounce of the game, the atmosphere filled with a sound like thunder as the crowd rose to their feet. Dylan launched himself to tap the ball.

Pain shot through his body like a lightning bolt, and he jerked away from the ball mid-air and landed awkwardly in the middle of the scrum. Eyes closed, mouth open in silent agony, he held his thigh as he rolled to his side. He could hear the grunts and calls around him as everyone scrambled for the ball, then felt jostled as a body landed beside him.

"Dude, what hurts? Talk to me."

"Got a corky." Dylan said through clenched teeth. Someone rolled him onto his back and disengaged his hands from his thigh.

"I thought so. I saw the mongrel dig his boot in as he went up for the ball."

He recognized Jason's voice, and let his teammate compress the area. He covered his face with his arms. He'd only corked a thigh once before, and it hadn't hurt this much.

He growled as the pain radiated up and down his leg.

"The medics are on their way, big fella. Think you'll be out for the rest of this game. It looks bad already."

"Thanks." Dylan coughed and tried to roll onto his side, but Jason held him where he was. Within moments, he heard the medics come alongside him. In one painful motion, they had him off the ground, on the stretcher, and loaded onto the medic cart.

The sports doctor and physiotherapist met him on the boundary line to assess the damage. Within minutes, he was aided off the ground for immediate treatment.

The roar of the crowd above the clubroom was like rubbing salt on a raw wound. Dylan lay on the massage table, leg elevated in a compression bandage, ice pack in hand to apply for twenty minutes every two hours. He rubbed his temples. The painkillers had kicked in and he was feeling a little drowsy, but not so drowsy as to not realize he had underestimated his opponent and run in without doing his homework first.

"Great start to the season," he muttered to himself.

"Ok, Dylan." Steven Price, the sports doctor entered the room. "I've organized an appointment at the hospital for x-rays to ensure there are no femoral fractures, but I'm fairly confident you've sustained a moderate quadriceps contusion and will require a good seventy-two hours of RICE and No HARM treatments. I'd also like you perform light stretches as soon as you can, and see me on Tuesday for another assessment. We'll work out your rehabilitation program from there."

Steven flipped his folder closed and tucked it under his arm as if he'd just invited Dylan over for dinner. Dylan wanted to be thankful, but he felt a scowl spreading over his face. The man was all matter-of-fact and no sympathy.

"Can I play next week?"

"We will assess that on Tuesday, but I highly doubt it. I suspect you'll be out for a minimum of two weeks."

Dylan blinked. He'd only just started to play. "Anything I can do to hurry up the healing?"

"Just do what is asked. The ambulance will be here in five minutes to pick you up. Make sure that when you are at home, you rest. Keep that leg elevated." With a quick rap on Dylan's shoulder, Steven left the clubrooms.

"See you Tuesday."

# THIRTY-SEVEN

Dylan stared at the lounge room ceiling. It was filthy. Dust tinted the fourteen-foot pressed tin ceiling, and cobwebs drooped about the cornices. While he rarely spent time in the lounge room, he was still disappointed in himself for not having noticed and cleaned the ceiling.

A corky meant three days of strict rest with his leg elevated. Dylan shook his head. Coach Davis would have had him back on the field in the second half. What was he going to do for three whole days if he was only allowed to get up to do light exercises and stretches?

The idea of picking up his Bible studies again crossed his mind. It had been months since he'd last opened the devotional, but the idea was quickly thrown out as he heard a car pull up in the drive. It stopped, Jack's voice become audible. Dylan pushed himself up on the couch and craned his neck to look outside, but he couldn't see over the window ledge. Who was visiting? Jack never mentioned the people he knew, so Dylan had no idea. The front door opened, and a muffled conversation spilled into the hallway. He slipped back into the couch to listen.

Dylan couldn't make out more than one or two words. But he could pick up the tone, and the tone wasn't friendly. It was like the hushed voices in study period before an exam: nervous and unsure. The front door closed, the car started, and the sound of footsteps disappeared down the hall. Moments later, Jack appeared in the lounge room doorway. Dylan couldn't tell if his expression was one of surprise or fear.

"How long have you been here?" he asked, his claw-like fingers gripping the doorframe.

Dylan raised his eyebrows. "I live here, remember."

"I mean, in the house," Jack said.

"Twenty-three years." If he wasn't so bored, he'd have answered his brother's question properly. But he needed entertainment. Besides, Jack never gave him straight answers. Unable to help himself, he grinned at Jack's obvious irritation. When Jack entered the room, Dylan felt his grin drop away.

"How long have you been in the house, today?" Jack's tone was dangerously calm.

Dylan remembered Jack's strength last time he'd cornered him. Time to stop his game. While he'd be more than willing to take on his brother in a fair fight, he was injured. Imagine what Coach Carter and Steven Price would say.

"I laid on the couch about 10 minutes ago, Jack. Before that, I was in my room. Relax."

Jack held his gaze for a moment longer before backing out of the room and disappearing from the doorway. A heavy sensation swirled within Dylan as he took a deep breath in through his nose, then blew it out his mouth. If only he could have seen the other person or heard a word of their conversation. Then he might be able to give Nick a few more clues.

\* \* \*

"Knock, knock."

Trent's voice in the empty house was like a breath of fresh air. Dylan threw down his magazine. "In the lounge room."

"Want anything from the kitchen while I'm in here?"

Dylan smiled. "Yeah. A bottle of water and an apple. Thanks, mate."

Moments later Trent appeared and tossed the items to him as he took a seat on the armchair adjacent to the couch. "How the recovery going?

"I'm going mad."

Trent laughed, and Dylan chucked in response. "I'm serious. I've never had to sit still for so long."

"Well, brother, least you're spending some time around home."

Jack had rarely been home and never said where he was going or when he'd be back. Mum was in and out all day, returning with more garden ornaments and ideas for the garden. But he couldn't deny there was a light in her eyes now.

"You're right. Mum's happier I'm home a bit more."

The afternoon passed quickly with Trent's company, and Dylan enjoyed listening to what had been happening since his life had rocketed into the fast lane. He smiled as Trent told him about how youth was going and the different things Dave had them doing, along with the monthly socials. He was happy the leadership team had carried on without a hiccup since he'd had to leave. Maybe he'd try to get a Friday night off and put in a cameo visit. The youth would love that.

When Trent asked how things were going at home, it took a weight off his shoulders to be able to fill Trent in what had been happening with Jack. "He needs prayers, mate. Something is very wrong with him and I don't really want to consider what my instincts are telling me."

"I pray for him every day," Trent said, his voice solemn and expression intent. "But sometimes the lesson the individual needs to learn is in the pain."

"That's what I'm worried about." Dylan readjusted himself on the couch. "I've spoken to Nick about him, but the girls don't know what's going on. I'd like to keep it that way for the moment. Is that cool?"

"It's not my business to tell. You tell the girls whenever you want to."

It was almost dinner time before Trent looked at the clock above the mantel and called it a day.

"I need to swing by Hope's on the way home to see how she's going."

Dylan rose and slowly walked Trent to the kitchen to collect his things he'd left on the dining table. "Thanks for coming, man. You've made the day fly."

"Anytime."

They stepped outside, and Dylan saw Jack over by the shed. He hummed in thought. "I didn't think Jack was home."

"Might be a good idea to spend some time with him," Trent said as he headed for his car. "Even if he pushes you away, least you know—and he knows— you've tried."

As the dust settled over the driveway after Trent left, Dylan decided to go see what Jack was up to. The fact alone that Jack was in the shed was interesting. Jack never went near the shed.

With measured steps, Dylan worked his way over to the shed when the thought flew into his mind that Jack might pawn his bike for money. A shot of anxiety flushed his system and weakened his legs at the thought. Dylan hurried his pace. Surely Jack wouldn't dare ...

"Hey, Jack," Dylan called out, his chest tight in the wake of the unnerving thought about his bike. "What are you up too?"

"Just looking for something," Jack said, not turning to look at him.

As Dylan entered the shed, he looked over his bike. It appeared untouched but the thought of it being stolen had rocked him as much as if it actually had been. He ran a hand over the seat and up to the handlebars. "What are you looking for? Can I help?"

Jack turned to him and huffed as he pushed his unruly hair back. It was greasy and needed a wash. "No. I don't need your help, and it's none of your business what I'm looking for."

"There's no need for the attitude—"

"Then just leave me alone!" Jack turned back to the boxes in the back of the shed.

Dylan's felt his jaw clench. "Perhaps I would leave you alone if you hadn't been behaving so crazy the last couple of months. What's going on with you?"

Jack whirled around. Dylan stood up to his full height, ready for whatever might come. Jack stopped in front of him, the same black look filled his eyes that Dylan had seen moments before Jack lunged at him in the kitchen.

"There ... is ... nothing ... wrong ... with ... me," Jack said through his teeth, poking a bony finger in Dylan's chest. Dylan batted the hand away.

"Bull! You look terrible. A strong breeze would blow you away. You're not fooling anyone."

Jack turned to leave the shed, but Dylan caught the crook of his arm and turned him back to him. "Look, whatever is going on –"

"There is nothing going on!" Jack shoved at Dylan with his free hand. This time, it felt like a feather brushing against him, and Dylan let him go. He couldn't risk injuring himself further. But if he didn't do something soon, he feared what might happen to his brother, and their family.

His phone pinged with a message, and he pulled it from his back pocket. Trent.

*'Hey bro, just wondering. Was Jack in the house today? I'm missing some money from my wallet.'*

# THIRTY-EIGHT

"Just as I thought." Steven Price ran a large, well-formed hand over Dylan's thigh. "You'll miss two weeks."

The clubrooms were cool, and brilliant sunbeams shone through the upper windows as Dylan lay on his back on the treatment table. There was still a hint of liniment in the air from the weekend game, but mostly he could smell the scent of cut grass from the ground maintenance crew working outside. It reminded him of lazy weekends, working outside with Dad.

Dylan sucked in a breath, raising himself up he watched as Steven worked the corked area of his thigh deeply. "That's a bit hard, Steve."

"Get used to it," Steven said, not lightening the pressure." If you want this thigh to be as loose at the other, we have to break down the clotted blood and realign the healing muscle fibers."

Dylan lowered himself back onto the table. Two weeks off. He felt flat. "So what do I do for the next two weeks?"

"In the first week, you'll have physiotherapy and massages in place of training sessions. Then you'll rejoin the training sessions in week two, along with continuing physiotherapy and massage treatments. We'll reassess your fitness for the next fortnight's game on Thursday week. It's up to you if you attend the games or not. Many players attend the games as moral support for their teammates."

As corellas and magpies called from the gum trees outside the clubrooms, Dylan stared the ceiling and sighed heavily. So much for a great start to the season. "When's my next appointment?"

"I'll give you a timetable before you leave today, and some exercises to do at home." Steve said. "Roll over."

After an hour of agonizing massage and painful stretches, Dylan limped towards the car park with his recovery timetable in hand.

When he reached the family car, Mum was reading a magazine. She reached across the seat and pushed the door open for him. He'd been advised not to ride his bike because of the extent of his injury. Being driven wherever he needed to go added to his depressed mood—he loved his bike.

"Where to now?" Mum asked, her voice as crisp as the birds calling in the trees above.

"Home, I guess." Dylan pulled on his seatbelt.

"Home it is." She pointed the car out of the car park. "I was thinking, if you're not too sore maybe you could help me in the garden this afternoon."

He'd be happy with that, as long as it wasn't building another gnome village. "Sure, Mum. No worries."

As they approached their house, they passed a police car coming the other way. The officer waved as he passed, and Dylan returned the gesture. He was thankful the police had agreed to his request to have regular drive-bys since their house had been raided. Even though he was going to be home more over the next two weeks, he was still thankful for it. The idea of Jack being involved in a drug cartel gave him chills.

Once Mum had parked the car, Dylan climbed out and moved to the rear of the car to help her with the shopping. She waved him away.

"I don't need you yet. Besides, you're meant to be resting. Get inside and I'll bring you a sandwich for lunch."

As Dylan slipped onto the couch and switched the TV on, his phone beeped. Yawning, he pulled the phone from his pocket and checked the message.

*'Thought I'd try to cheer Hope up by taking her out for her birthday. You free Thursday night? BTW, saw the corky you copped. Damn! Josh.'*

Dylan grinned. He was free, and a night out with good company was just what he needed. He hit reply.

*'Yeah, wasn't good. I'm out for two weeks. I'm free Thursday. What do you have in mind?'*

Mum came in with a sandwich and glass of water for him, bright smile on her face. She put the items on the coffee table, and left. His phone buzzed.

*'Dinner in the city. Meet us at Southbank Marina. We're doing a river diner cruise.'*

Dylan's eyebrows shot up. He hit reply and reached for his sandwich.

*'Nice! Sure you kids won't want to be alone?'*

"Sweetie." Mum reappeared in the doorway. "I'm heading out to the garden. I have my phone if you need anything."

Dylan laughed. "Mum, I'm not crippled. I have a corked thigh. I'll be out shortly to give you a hand."

As he settled back in the couch to finish his lunch, his phone went off again. Josh again. He read the message and chuckled.

*'We will be alone afterwards ;) See you Thursday at seven.'*

A few more bites and he'd finished the sandwich, and the water was gone with a few gulps. Dylan stood, stretched out his thigh again, and made his way outside to help Mum while thoughts of Thursday night played over in his mind.

A dinner river cruise …

He stepped onto the back lawn and Mum looked up at him from where she was digging, over by the drooping willow trees. She had dirt smeared on her forehead, but her eyes were shinning as she sat back on her heels.

"I want to put in a water fountain and pond over here, and a bench seat." She pointed to the area in front of her. "And I thought these petunias would add a bit of color."

"Sounds great, Mum. What do you want me to do?"

"Just keep me company." She brushed a fly away, smearing another streak of dirt over her forehead.

"I can do that." Dylan lowered himself to the grass and stretched out in the sun, enjoying the heat on his skin and the smell of flowers and dirt filling his senses.

The upcoming dinner cruise played over in his mind, filling him with energy. It would be the perfect setting for him to have a much-needed quiet conversation with Lexi about where she was at. He knew things were positive from her reaction at the movie night, he'd hardly seen her in the last few months since his new career took off. A lot could change in three months.

He prayed things hadn't. He missed her.

# THIRTY-NINE

"*D*ylan speaking."

Dylan pressed the speaker button on his phone and continued dressing for the dinner cruise. He'd even gone out and bought a new shirt and cologne. The sales assistant had suggested a popular cologne brand, saying the low notes—whatever that was—of sensual leather and cedar wood wouldn't disappoint. It better not, considering the cost.

"Dylan, its Lachlan Ward. How are you doing, son?"

Why would the club president call him? He finished pulling his shirt on. "I'm well, thank you sir. What can I do for you?"

A soft chuckle came down the line. "Call me Lachlan, remember?"

Dylan took the phone off speaker and sat on the end of his bed. "Ok, Lachlan, what can I do for you?"

"Son, I have a huge opportunity for you. The live National Football Show has requested you to join them on the discussion panel tonight. I know its short notice, but this is a sensational opportunity for your career. It's unprecedented for a new recruit to be asked onto the program so early in the season, so I highly recommend you accept. What do you say? You busy?"

Dylan felt his spirits sore moments before reality crashed over him. He looked at his bedside clock. He was meant to be at the Southbank Marina in less than two hours.

"Dylan?" Lachlan's voice came down the line, patient but expecting in its tone.

"Yeah, I'm here," Dylan said. "I do have a prior engagement."

"This opportunity doesn't come up often. As you can imagine, there are a number of players out there who would do anything to lift their profiles by being on this show. Is your prior engagement more important that this?"

Dylan rubbed his jaw and looked out his bedroom window. He did know. He also knew his friends would be disappointed in him. He cleared his throat. "You're right. Sorry. I can reschedule. I accept the offer. Where do you want me to meet you and at what time?"

As Dylan listened to Lachlan explain the evening ahead, a twinge of excitement sparked within him. He'd watched the National Football Show since he was a boy, and never imagined he'd be asked to be on the panel one day. His friends would understand.

Lachlan ended the phone call, and Dylan quickly changed into what Lachlan had instructed him to wear, then called Josh to let him know he couldn't make it. The call went to voicemail, and Dylan left a message explaining what had happened, wished them a good night and that he'd catch up with them another time.

Happy with his appearance, he patted some of the new cologne onto his face, then went to find Mum to arrange a lift into the city. His phone rang. It was Lachlan again.

"Hello, Lachlan." Dylan hoped he wasn't calling to cancel his appearance tonight.

"Dylan, I've arranged a car for you into and out from the city. It will be there within ten minutes. See you soon, son."

The line when dead, and Dylan stared at his phone. Were all new players treated like this? Before he could get his head around what was happening, a horn tooted from outside their home. Snagging his suit jacket off the edge of his bed, he hobbled to the front door. Mum stood in the doorway, confusion marking her features.

"Hey, Mum. Sorry, I can't explain now." Dylan planted a quick kiss on her cheek. "Gotta run. But make sure you watch our favorite footy show tonight."

As he hastened towards the sleek limousine idling in their driveway, Dylan swung his jacket on and smoothed his hair back. This was a dream.

Totally a dream.

Just over an hour later, the vehicle pulled up to a gated parking area. After a short pause, the gates opened before them and the car rolled forward. Once the car parked, Dylan turned to open his door but it was opened for him. He stepped out into what looked to be a rear of stage area. After thanking the chauffeur, Dylan buttoned up his suit jacket and he moved towards an open door. Light and sound spilled out.

Lachlan met him just inside the door and shook his hand firmly. After a quick chat, an assistant hurried him to the dressing rooms, and he was soon face to face with the other players who would be on the panel tonight. Doug McLaren and Tony Adamson, two of the biggest players in the league.

Dylan shook their hands. Both greeted him warmly and by name.

"How do you fellas know me?" Dylan asked, taking a seat as instructed by the hairdresser.

"Think you'll find everyone has heard of the new recruits," Doug said. "It's great to meet you."

"We do our homework too," Tony added.

Before he could say anything, the show's producer entered the dressing room and gave them a rundown of what was going to be discussed, things they were not to comment on, and what time they were expected to finish up. Dylan's head was spinning. He could hear the live audience filling the stands and the tech crew calling to each other for last-minute sound checks. But when he, Doug, and Tony were asked to get ready for when they'd be called out onto the panel, his stomach dropped.

Live television.

He was about to be on live television.

"Don't pass out, son." Doug pounded his back. "You'll have a lot of fun. Just be yourself."

Dylan gave the man a thumbs up, feigning a coolness he was far from feeling. His heart raced, his hands were clammy, and his mouth was dry. Was there any water? A backstage worker appeared from nowhere and thrust a bottle into his hand, then offered one to Tony and one to Doug.

The ON AIR sign above him came on and he blew his breath out.

Moments later, Doug was introduced and the audience roared.

Dylan hopped on the spot.

Tony was called out, and the audience cheered and clapped with excitement.

Dylan sculled his water and shook his arms out.

His name was called, and everything became white noise, moving in slow motion as he stepped out onto the stage to a roar of applause. This must be a dream.

Totally a dream.

# FORTY

Dylan opened an eye. What was that noise?

His room was dully illuminated. Morning was on its way. With a wide yawn, he turned his bedside clock towards him to see what time it was.

5:47 am.

With a groan Dylan rolled onto his back. Three hours sleep was not—

There it was again.

In one fluid motion, Dylan threw back his covers and launched himself out of bed. Maybe the neighbor's pigs had escaped. Maybe Jack was watching a movie. No. He pulled on a pair of tracksuit pants and quietly left his room.

"Dear God, please let Mum not have heard what I heard," Dylan muttered quietly.

He pushed open Jack's door. The dim light showed Jack in the bed. And someone else. The figures stilled and the sheets settled over them. Jaw clenched, Dylan waited, not believing the scene before him. As the sun peaked over the horizon and speared the room with light, Jack's head appeared from under the sheets.

Unfocussed red eyes glared at him from sunken sockets, his skin pale and lifeless even in the rosy early morning light. The sheets rustled again and a young female looked back at him. She was as pale as Jack, and must have been no more than fifteen.

Repercussions crashed in Dylan's mind at the scene before him, though he swallowed his infuriation and took a deep breath.

"Leave." He opened the door and glared at the young girl. She threw the sheets back, leapt from the bed despite Jack's protests, and scuttled past Dylan. She moved fast. The screen door banged shut moments later, telling Dylan she was gone. He continued to glower at Jack, barely believing what he'd seen.

As Jack pushed himself up, Dylan pulled the door closed and stalked outside. He wanted to get as far from the house as possible, conscious of Mum asleep inside and not trusting himself to speak with Jack peacefully.

"Hey!"

Dylan stopped at Jack's shout and turned, irritated. Jack was heading towards him, his gait unbalanced.

He'd had the time of his life last night. Lachlan had told him his appearance on the show had lifted the viewer stats and hits on their club website. But to come home to this ... His muscles tensed.

He remained silent as Jack stopped, inches from him, and glared at him with unblinking, glazed eyes.

"What do you think you're doing, coming into my room?" Jack said, just managing to keep breaks between the words of his sentence. Dylan took a step back in an unsuccessful attempt to get away from Jack's repugnant odor, and screwed his face up in reaction to the smell.

Jack poked a finger into his chest. "Answer me!"

Dylan slapped his brother's hand away, and stepped towards him, ignoring the stench. "Don't you dare speak to me like that," he said, careful to keep his voice down. "You are nineteen years old and had an underage girl in your bed. Be thankful I didn't leave you to it and call the police." Disgusted, Dylan turned from Jack and let out a frustrated growl as he linked his hands behind his head. What a mess.

"As if you'd do that." Jack's scoffing voice came from behind him.

Dylan dropped his arms to his side. "How old is she?"

Jack's voice held a note of contempt. "Relax. She's old enough."

"How long has this been going on?" He turned, wanting to watch Jack answer the question. He could pick a liar, and Jack knew it.

Jack sniffed and looked away.

"Don't answer that." Dylan said quickly. A heavy sensation formed in his gut. "Listen, I know you're into some messed-up things, but—"

"What makes you think I'm on something?" Jack snarled, closing the distance between them. "Like you have any idea of what's going on around this place. You're never here!"

Dylan breathed through his mouth. The stench of Jack's body odor mixed with alcohol and sweat was turning his stomach. "My absence is no green light to play up. Do you have any idea of what you're messing with? Mum would be so disappointed. Dad would turn in his grave!"

Jack grinned a slow, wicked grin dripping with mockery as he swayed then took a step backwards. "She doesn't know what day it is, let alone what I'm doing. Besides, it's none of your business, and it's definitely none of hers."

Dylan grabbed Jack's shirt and pulled his brother into his chest, pinning him with all his bottled-up anger. "Listen, you little punk, it is my business if it means you bring disgrace to our family or hurt somebody with your negligence. Now, smarten up!"

Dylan shoved Jack away. Blood thumped through his veins, and his muscles twitched. "Who was that girl, anyway?"

"Jealous, are you?" Jack regained his footing and managed to stay upright. "That I have a girl and you don't?"

"Far from it, Jack. You're a disgrace. Are you even aware of what you're playing with?"

"What's it to you?" Jack swayed again. "I'll do what I like, when I like, and with who I like."

Dylan swallowed what he really wanted to say and forced himself to think clearly. He had to get Jack to spill some clues he could pass onto Nick. And quickly, before he ran out of time. Judging by the rapid way Jack was deteriorating before his eyes, that would be soon. He'd get thrown in prison, overdose, or get himself killed.

Dylan took a deep breath. "I'm not trying to parent you, but I do know you're playing with drugs. Blind Freddy could—"

Jack came at Dylan with such speed that Dylan was caught off guard and the blackness that flashed behind Jacks eyes again, sent a stab of fear into his heart.

"If I have to tell you once more that there is nothing wrong with me …"

"You'll what? I'm already all over you like a rash, buddy. Any day now, your little game will be up."

Jack shoved at him once, twice, three times, grunting and screaming. To Dylan's relief, Jack barely moved him. Thankfully, whatever had possessed Jack that day in the kitchen was hopefully gone. Dylan grabbed his brother's wrists and tried to calm him. When he became manic, Dylan let him go. If he didn't, he might hurt him. Instead, Dylan watched as Jack staggered back towards the house, cursing as he went.

Seeing Jack like this both terrified and angered Dylan, and a sense of helplessness engulfed him like a fog on the ocean. There was no way out. He was completely lost. Turning his gaze skyward, he started to pour his heart out to God for help.

But one final shout from Jack revealed a threat that made his blood run cold.

Jack was after his bike.

# FORTY-ONE

"Nick, man, you're a lifesaver." Dylan locked his bike, then stepped out of the shed and watched as Nick pulled the garage door down and punched in the security code.

"Don't mention it. He sounds like he's getting desperate if he's going to pawn your bike," Nick said.

"I'd say he is."

"Was your mum able to give you any details on the two goons who came to your house that night?"

"No. She gets all worked up when I ask her, so I don't want to try again. I get the feeling she's skating on thin ice too." Dylan rubbed the back of his neck.

Nick mm-ed in agreement. "Is she talking to Lexi?"

"Mum's told me that she's chewed Lexi's ear off a few times."

Nick chuckled. "I'm surprised Lexi hasn't bailed you up over it yet."

Dylan blew his breath out. "I'm not. I saw the way she looked at me at the movie night. She probably thinks I've got something going on with Hope now."

Dylan plunged his hands into his pockets and leaned against the rendered bricks of Nick's family home and glanced at his friend.

"Pretty much."

"What?" Dylan asked, pushing himself off the wall and turning to face Nick.

"Well, what did you expect? It's not like you made an obvious attempt to move away from Hope that night. Then Hope's outburst at her birthday when Josh said you weren't coming didn't help."

Dylan stared at Nick. What was going on with Hope? "Look, I don't know what you're talking about, but there is nothing between Hope and me." It was the truth, but would Nick believe him?

When Nick didn't say anything, Dylan shook his head and turned away. Every corner of his life was practically perfect not even a year ago, and now there were issues wherever he looked. How was that possible?

"I'm just telling you what I know," Nick said, breaking the silence. "How she was all over you at the movie night then flipped when you didn't come to her party. Maybe you need to talk to Hope."

"No, I'm going to talk to Lexi," Dylan said, "This is getting ridiculous! The café is just a couple blocks up, so I'll walk. Thanks again for locking up my bike. I owe you."

Nick clapped him on the shoulder. "Just get me some more information so we can nail these guys Jack's involved with. Good luck with Lexi."

"Thanks. I've got a feeling I'm going to need it."

* * *

Thankful his leg was starting to improve, Dylan strode through the shopping center towards the food court to speak with Lexi. She had the afternoon shift on Friday, but he couldn't wait until she was free to have this conversation. He had to clear the air. Today. Now.

As he entered the food court, he fixed his eyes on the Ocean View Café and was heading towards it when a handful of young kids stepped into his path.

"Hey, Dylan! I saw you last night."

"Are you ok? I saw you get injured. Can you play this week?"

"Can you sign my t-Shirt? Really big?"

Dylan looked up from the gathered young people to the café and caught Lexi glance his way while working on an order. The smile on her face didn't lighten her features when their eyes met, and his stomach dropped. A tap on his arm brought his attention back to his fans. "I'm sorry, guys. Of course, I'll sign your things."

As Dylan signed what they handed him, he answered their questions and felt his spirit lift a little. He excused himself from the children, not wanting to hang around for small talk, and pulled a chair up at the café just as Lexi finished taking payment for an order. She looked over at him as she flipped a tea towel over her shoulder.

"Hey," she said. Her tone was cool, and she kept her distance.

Dylan didn't want that to discourage him, so he launched straight into what he wanted to talk about.

"Hey, Lex. Sorry to bother you at work but I've just come from Nick's and he said you're upset about a couple of things."

She tucked a stay hair behind her ear. "What? No. I'm fine."

"Where Hope is concerned…"

Lexi shrugged, shook her head, then pulled the towel off her shoulder and worked a nonexistent mark on the counter. "Hope? Oh, the movie night thing? I spoke to her about that. It's cool."

Lexi's lack of eye contact told him she was uncomfortable with the conversation and suggested she wasn't being honest with him. "And the birthday party …"

She glanced up at him, and he caught a flash of hesitation behind her eyes. "What about the birthday party?"

"Lexi," Dylan said, his gaze steady. "I'm not interested in Hope."

Her cheeks flamed with color as the counter bell chimed, but she didn't look away.

"I don't know what's going on with Hope, but I need you to know there's nothing there on my end."

The counter bell chimed again. When the customer cleared his throat in an exaggerated manner, Dylan broke their connection and glanced at the waiting customer then back at Lexi. Her eyes were downcast as she toyed with the tea towel in her hands. When she looked back up at him, he tried to convey the need he felt to reassure her through his eyes. "Are we cool?"

"Excuse me, miss. Can I get some service over here?"

Lexi shuttered her expression and turned to the customer. "Sorry, sir, I won't be a moment." When she turned back to him, Dylan watched her straighten out her apron with shaky hands and waited for her to speak.

"I gotta get back to work." Lexi said after a moment, her pulse visible in her neck.

Dylan drew in a deep breath and blew it out. "Yeah."

She hesitated a moment, then moved to serve the waiting customer. Frustrated at knowing the issue wasn't resolved, Dylan watched her for a moment before leaving quietly. He strode from the food court, allowing his thoughts to move to his recovery. He had to concentrate on getting himself better so he could play next week. One week off was enough.

Adrenaline began pumping at the thought of running onto the field next week. Adam was hosting the Friday night team-building session and he wanted nothing more than a stress-free evening.

# FORTY-TWO

"You are right to play."

Those were some of the best words Dylan had ever heard. With a long sigh of relief, he tilted his head back and smiled up at the sky. "Thank you!"

"No need to thank me," Steven Price said as he packed up his things. "You've done everything right, and your body has healed well. The only reason I'm am surprised is because this injury generally takes a minimum of two weeks to come good."

Dylan grinned, throwing another glance skyward and inwardly thanking God for his rapid healing. "So I'm right to participate in today's training?"

"Take things slow, but yes. Just so you know, I'll be suggesting to Coach Carter that you only play two quarters on the weekend, and he's to call you off if you appear to be tiring at any stage."

"Understood." Dylan shook Steven's hand and watched as he left the room. Only when the door shut behind him did Dylan let out a shout for joy. He got up off the table, collected his things, then made his way out to join the boys in their training drills.

It was a sight for sore eyes. The boundary line filled with supporters, flags waving, his teammates passing footballs to one another, Coach Carter's voice booming over the grounds. All of it. It was like he had been away for weeks. Moving from a brisk walk to a slow jog, Dylan closed in on his team and couldn't help but smile when a few of the boys saw him approach, broke training, and cheered, welcoming him back.

He felt good. His legs felt strong, and his fitness hadn't diminished in his ten days of rest thanks to the rigorous physiotherapy sessions. Now, seated in the clubrooms, listening to the rundown for the weekend's game, he felt focused. His mind was sharp. When Coach told him who he was up against, he made a mental note to do his homework this time.

As far as Dylan was concerned, the rest of the week couldn't go fast enough. Just two more sleeps and he'd be running out with his teammates to do battle once more.

* * *

Passing a patrolling police car on the way home was becoming the norm. But turning into the driveway of the family home and seeing flashing ambulance lights was the making of nightmares. Dylan's heart kicked into double time and he leaned forward over the steering wheel, trying to see better as he approached the house, yet not sure if he wanted to see why medics were gathering at his home.

With a prayer for guidance, Dylan parked Mum's car, then quickly made his way inside to find the window above the sink had been smashed, and several dining chairs lay in pieces around the room. Mum sat on the only chair left and while her arm was in a sling, it was the cut mark along her neck that made him feel sick. She was surrounded by police constables taking notes and ambulance crew taking observations. He started to shake.

An ambulance officer moved into his vision and Dylan snapped back into the moment, unaware of how long he'd been standing in the hallway.

"Son?" The ambulance officer said. "Can I help you?"

Dylan focused on the older man before him. He had kind brown eyes and looked to be strong despite his age. He was about to answer the question when Mum started sobbing.

"Dylan! Is that you? Dylan please…"

Dylan stepped past the officer and went to his Mum. Her fierce hug knocked the wind out of him. Her fingers clawed into his sides, and he felt every uneven breath she took. Most of the police officers in the kitchen left quietly, leaving one with note-pad in hand and pen poised. A single ambulance officer remained, checking Mum's blood pressure. He cleared his throat, unsure how his voice would sound.

"What happened here?"

Before anyone could answer, Mum let out another wail and held onto him even harder.

The heart rate monitor beeped rapidly. The Ambulance officer approached, whispered quietly in her ear, and eased her arms from around Dylan. What had happened? The police officer led Dylan from the kitchen and into the quiet of the lounge room.

"I assume you're the son she keeps asking for?" The police officer said. Dylan nodded, and the man held a hand out to him. "I'm Senior Sergeant Barker. My partner, Leading Constable White, and I responded to the triple-zero call of domestic disturbance from this address about forty-five minutes ago."

"Domestic disturbance, sir?" Dylan said, almost choking as the words passed over his tongue.

Senior Sergeant Barker made a motion towards the couch. Dylan sat, needing no encouragement.

"I'm not sure if you are aware or not, but your brother is known to the police. We believe he has been involved in a number of offenses including robbery, assault, and theft, although we don't have enough evidence to charge him yet. His name has recently been dropped as a possible drug trafficker too."

Dylan ran a hand over his hair and sank back into the couch, blowing his breath out. "No, I didn't know this. When did he appear on your radar?"

"When he was sixteen."

Dylan swallowed hard—three years ago, not long after Dad died. "Ok. What happened here tonight?"

"Drug-induced aggravated assault. Your mother says Jack was agitated all afternoon, then snapped this evening when he asked for money and she wouldn't give him any. She says he held a knife to her throat, but something caused him to drop the knife and run from the house."

Dylan stood and paced the room. Everything was entirely too hard to get his head around. "What happens now?"

"We have a search warrant out for his arrest, and we will be in touch when we find him."

The other ambulance officer entered the room and asked to speak privately with Senior Sergeant Barker. Without a word, Dylan got up and made his way back into the kitchen. He lifted himself onto the bench, and sat quietly with Mum.

How was life ever meant to return to normal?

# FORTY-THREE

Lachlan Ward relaxed into his high-back leather chair and steepled his fingers. "How is your Mum this morning?"

"They want her to stay in one more night." Dylan said. Just explaining to his boss what had happened last night sounded like he was relaying the plot of a bad movie. "They had her on some pretty strong meds to calm her down when I went to see her this morning. Apparently, she had some nightmares last night."

Lachlan hummed, his gaze intent. "Dylan, I think its best we pull you from the game tomorrow—"

Dylan sat forward in his seat, unsure he'd heard correctly. Missing another game on top of everything else that was going on was the last straw, but Lachlan held up his hand in a signal for silence.

"I'm sorry son, but my mind is made up."

You've got bigger things to worry about this weekend. I can't risk having you on field and not concentrating. You'll wind up putting yourself and your teammates in jeopardy."

Dylan sank back in his chair and his arms fell heavily onto his lap as he looked out the office window. There was no point arguing. The big boss had already made the call.

Lachlan moved to perch on the edge of his desk. "I'm not saying your contract is cancelled, son. It's just one game. Besides, one more week off will ensure that leg injury of yours will heal properly."

Lachlan was trying to offer Dylan some encouragement, and it would be ungracious of him to not acknowledge that. He stood and offered his hand to Lachlan. "As much as I want to play, I understand where you're coming from."

"Your family and your health are the most important things at this time. Take care of them." Lachlan said. His voice warm and fatherly. Dylan hung his head, swallowing resentment like it was vinegar in his mouth. He forced a neutral expression as he looked up and ended the meeting. "I will, sir."

"Good man." Lachlan rose from his desk and moved towards the door. Dylan followed his lead. "Enjoy the rest of your day, son."

As Dylan walked out of the Condors headquarters into the brilliant morning sunshine, he wasn't sure if he wanted to cry or hit something. Issues with Jack had curbed his decisions for years, and now they were forcing decisions—decisions made by others which affected him. He was at the end of his rope with Jack. If the cop's didn't do something about him soon, he would.

* * *

Dylan turned into his driveway to find Lexi's Jeep parked outside the family home. He gripped the steering wheel. "God, not now. Not. Now."

He parked the car under the peppercorn tree beside the house, snagged his sports bag from the back seat, and stepped out at the same time as Lexi stepped out from her car.

She moved towards him and paused by the verandah steps. "Thought you'd have been home, relaxing."

Dylan stopped opposite her and lifted the sports bag onto his shoulder. She seemed hesitant. "Had a pre-game meeting at the club this morning."

"How'd it go?" Lexi asked, an air of reluctance about her.

"I got scratched."

A flash of sadness crossed her features. "I'm sorry."

Pity. Exactly what he didn't want. He wanted everyone out of his way so he could play the sport he'd always loved playing on the platform he'd finally reached to play it.

"Thanks," he muttered as he turned to head up the steps. He looked over his shoulder. "What brings you out here?"

"I need to talk to you." Lexi followed him up the steps.

He dropped his sports bag beside the front door and gave her his full attention. "Ok. What's up?"

She toyed with her fingers and opened her mouth a couple of times, but didn't say anything. Instead, she fidgeted. Curiosity arose, and Dylan waited for her to find the words. An impish grin formed. Maybe she was going to start the conversation they both knew they needed to have.

"Here's the thing," Lexi said eventually, her fidgeting ceasing. "I'm worried about the direction you're headed in."

Dylan felt his grin turn into a smile as he crossed his arms. "And why's that?"

"Because I think football is becoming more than just a game to you."

A moment passed before her words registered and he frowned. "What?"

Lexi changed her weight from one side to the other. "Well, I've—no, we've all noticed that you've kind of disappeared. We hardly see you anymore and when we do, you're always far away somewhere in your head thinking of the next game. It's pretty much all you talk about, and the last time I saw you in church you were on your phone checking out football stuff. That's not like you."

Dylan blinked. "Lexi. Thank you, but I know what I'm doing."

"Yeah, I'm sure you do. I used to say the same thing, last year."

"Wait." Dylan held a hand up, needing a moment to get his head around what she was saying. "You're comparing me and my football career to you and that … that … whatshisname?"

"Well, yeah—" .

How could she say such a thing? "There is no comparison. That was a relationship; this is my career."

"I'm comparing the effects, not what they are," Lexi said gently, taking a small step towards him. "The comparison is that he got in the way of the most important things in my life, just like football is getting in the way in yours. And, just like I couldn't see it happening, I don't think you can see what's happening either."

Dylan took a step back from her and shook his head. "You have no have no idea what you're talking about. I know what goes on in my own home."

"Do you?" Lexi challenged, eyebrows raised.

Dylan plunged his hands into his pockets. "Yeah. I do."

"Do you really?"

"Yeah, I really do."

He always suspected Lexi had spunk, though had never seen her worked up enough to display it. Now, standing before him, jaw set, hands on her hips and blue eyes hard but brilliant in the midday sun, she wasn't backing down. However, nobody knew his household better than he did. He stepped past her and opened the screen door. This conversation was over.

She was beside him in a flash and pulled the front door shut then easing the screen door out of his hand, closed it as well and stood in his way. "Are you aware that your mother is having a nervous breakdown? She calls me all the time. She's crying, but I'm not allowed to say anything to you or anyone. Do you know how uncomfortable that makes me?"

"Yeah, I know." Dylan closed his eyes. He wished he could tell her what was going on.

"Are you also aware that your brother is not only on drugs, but dealing —" Lexi's tone turned accusing and the hairs on the back of Dylan's neck rose.

He opened his eyes and glowered back at her. "Lexi," he said, his tone warning.

"I'm talking ice, Dylan." Lexi snipped. "The heavy stuff. He's addicted."

"Yes, look, I—"

"Do you know about the underage girlfriend? Underage! That's statutory rape." Lexi's eyes flashed as she rose up on tip-toes as if to emphasis her point.

Dylan felt anger rise up within him. "Lexi, that's enough! I said I—"

"And I wonder who stole from Trent while he was visiting you? Coincidence?"

Jaw clenched, Dylan met Lexi's glare when she fell silent. There was so much he wanted to say. When, all of a sudden, his mind filled with thoughts of pressing her against the door and unleashing the desire for her that he had been suppressing. Her lips glistened with the strawberry lip balm she used, and were parted as if in invitation. He could almost feel her lips against his, almost feel her hair running through his fingers. His heart raced within his chest as his eyes fixed upon her mouth, and he battled his mind to refocus. He took a step back from her and caught his breath. She was flushed and her chest rose and fell shallowly.

Annoyed at himself, Dylan ran a hand over his hair and let his breath out slowly. "Look, I appreciate you worrying about me and my family, but it's in God's hands. He opened the door to this opportunity, so I'm trusting Him to take care of everything. It's an answered prayer, Lex. Everything will work out."

She pushed herself off the door and walked down the verandah steps, her knuckles white on the railing. He watched her, unsure what to say or if he should say anything. She stopped at her car door and turned back to him, the midday sun illuminating her auburn hair a fiery red.

"Dave delivered a really good youth message last month. He spoke about how both God and Satan have plans for our lives, and we need to be wise enough to know the difference between them."

What did she mean by that?

He jumped off the verandah and strode towards her car as she clicked her seatbelt in place and started the Jeep.

"Was there anything more to go with that? Or are you trying to tell me in a backwards way I've gone with Satan's plan, not God's?"

"We both know you didn't pray for this role. You prayed about captaincy for the Tigers. A role you were given ... but turned down. So it's up to you to figure out whose plan you're following."

Dylan stared down the driveway long after her Jeep had disappeared. What she said annoyed him. He knew he had fallen away from church and their youth group, but there were many ways to worship. He was worshiping through increasing the talent God had given him.

Wasn't he?

He frowned and shook his head, letting out a growl he ruffed up his hair and turned back to the house. It also annoyed him that he couldn't be completely honest and tell Lexi what was going on, but she had to stay in the dark until Jack was sorted.

Jack!

# FORTY-FOUR

With a single-minded intent, Dylan burst into Jack room. Whatever it took, he would find something in this mess today to take to Nick.

Unsure where to start, Dylan looked over the apocalyptic state of his brother's room. Where would he hide something if he didn't want a snooping mother or older brother to find? If this was one of those police shows Jack liked to watch, then Dylan would have to look deeper than under the clothes on the floor. Dylan stepped towards the wardrobe and opened it. He was going to find something if he had to rip open every seam of every piece of clothing, take every picture out of every frame, and shred the mattress. If nothing appeared from Jack's room, he would check the other rooms of the house.

Hours later, Dylan sat on the floor in his own room, gripping a list of names and addresses with today's date and some strange icon in the top right corner. The little punk had hidden something in his room!

Dylan shook his head and took a deep breath. He didn't know who he lived with, but it wasn't Jack. The younger brother who idolized him had died with Dad, and someone else had taken over.

*Well, that someone else was going down. Tonight.* Dylan pushed himself up and strode from his room, pulling the door shut behind him. After checking the kitchen clock, Dylan left a message for his mum saying he would be home late, and that tea would be delivered at seven-thirty.

As he jogged from the house, he pulled out his phone, dialed the local pizza place, and ordered tea to be delivered at seven-thirty.

\* \* \*

The door buzzer announced Dylan's entry into the Richmond Police Station, hoping to find Nick on duty. Nick wasn't responding to phone calls or messages, so the odds were good he was working. He approached the counter, pulled the crumpled flyer from his back pocket, and smoothed it over the desk. The reception door was opened and Nick stepped out.

"What brings you here?" Nick asked, resting a hip against the counter.

"Know anything about this?" Dylan pushed the flyer across the counter.

The door buzzed again, and Dylan glanced over his shoulder. Two young girls stumbled in, looking like they'd had a hard night. They'd started early—the night hadn't even begun. He acknowledged them, then turned back to Nick, his stomach dropped at the policeman's expression. Dylan asked the obvious question, not wanting to know the answer. "What? What is it?"

"Where did you get this?" Nick's eyes flashed.

"I found it in my room."

"Where?"

"Under the carpet."

Nick gave him a "really?" look, and Dylan rolled his eyes. "Yes, I ripped up my bedroom carpet. Why?"

Nick gestured to the far side of the counter as another officer entered and signaled to the girls to come forward. Dylan followed, a heavy sensation curling in his gut.

Nick sighed and handed the flyer back. "Listen, this is above me. But I can tell you the symbol in the swirling border here is a tag for one of the big drug runners in the city. How did Jack get invited to one of their parties?"

"I have my suspicions of how, but that's beside the point. I'm going to that party and I'm going—"

Nick held his hand up, and Dylan fell silent. When Nick withdrew what looked to be a large work diary, Dylan tilted his head to the side and tried to read what his mate was writing, but his scrawl-like handwriting made it difficult. Just as he started to put some words together, Nick flipped the book shut and thrust it back under the counter before turning back to Dylan. "Take a seat over there. I'll be right back."

His left leg twitched and nervous energy pooled in his gut as waited. Everything within him urged him to keep moving, and the hard plastic seats and lack of music playing in the reception area added to his anxiety. The room was becoming stuffy and the girls' dramatics at the front counter added to his irritation.

Why would Nick keep him waiting when time was ticking and every second counted? He'd give Nick two more minutes, then he'd be gone.

A door was ripped open in front of him, and an imposing form stepped out, the man's no-nonsense expression housing the most intense gaze Dylan had ever seen. When the man's steel-blue eyes zeroed in on him, Dylan's blood ran cold.

"Dylan Saunders?"

Dylan nodded. "Sir."

The man made a sharp head gesture into the room behind him. "This way."

Dylan swallowed hard and rubbed his sweaty palms on his thighs before he stood. Was he in trouble?

As he passed the man and stepped into the cold interview room, he caught his own concerned expression in the mirrored glass before him and stone-faced Nick standing in the corner behind him. Dylan sat, stretching his arms out on the table in front of him.

The imposing man closed the door then sat heavily at the table opposite Dylan and cleared his throat, his Adam's apple bobbing as he sorted papers in a file that lay in front of him. "Dylan, I am Sergeant Colton Derman. Constable Marshall here has been keeping me informed about your brother's activities. I understand you've found evidence linking your brother with a major drug cartel. We've been tracking this particular cartel for some time. Any idea how your brother became involved?"

Dylan shook his head. "Ah, not… really. He hangs around with a guy called Curt a fair bit."

"Surname? Sergeant Derman scrawled a note, not looking up.

"No. I've only seen him from far off. I just know Jack is into drugs from his recent behavior. There have also been some strange cars turn up at our place. But, they've been careful to stay in the shadows and not come too close. Also, one night when I came home late, there were two men at the house. They were looking for Jack." Dylan gave the sergeant a description of the two men.

"Did you happen to get the licence plate of that car?"

Dylan shook his head. "It was dark, and I just wanted to get inside to see what was going on."

Sergeant Derman tapped his pen on the paper he'd been making notes on. "I'm organizing an undercover team to go to this address tonight. Are you sure Jack will be there?"

Dylan shrugged. "That was where I was planning on going to find him."

The sergeant gave Dylan a stern look and a firm shake of the head. "No. That would be a bad idea. You've done the right thing by coming to the police. It'll be turned over to our undercover detectives. We have a picture on file of Jack—I assume you're aware of his activities?"

Dylan nodded. "Mum told me a police officer brought Jack home one night and filled her in on what he'd been up to."

Sergeant Derman coughed into his fist. "That was months ago, son. If we get our hands on Jack tonight, he's in a lot of trouble. He's got a list of offenses and they're growing by the day, no doubt to pay for the substances he's taking. We believe he's starting to get desperate. Robbery, aggravated assault, dealing in and with illegal substances. To date, Jack has managed to stay out of our grasp, but thanks to you, I think he'll be brought in tonight."

Dylan felt like he'd been punched in the stomach. He sat back in his chair and his arms fell limp in his lap. Sergeant Derman packed up the papers in front of him and put them neatly back in the file before looking at Dylan. "Thanks again, son. I suggest you head home. We'll call you when we have Jack."

Dylan scoffed inwardly. Sure, he'd just pop on home and have tea while he waited to hear how the bust on his brother went? He felt sick.

The door behind him opened. Time to go. Dylan nodded and rose. His eyes grazed Nick's as he headed out of the inter-view room and the silent exchange between them said more than words could.

Pray!

# FORTY-FIVE

Numb, Dylan watched the heart monitor track the slow steady rhythm of Jack's heart.

Moments before, the room had been filled with the chaotic action of doctors and nurses as they worked to stabilize their new patient. His brother. He'd watched from the corner of the room as orders where barked, notes taken, drips hooked up, and needles given. He'd turned away as a defibrillator was applied and cringed hearing life shocked back into his brother.

To think not even two hours ago, he was at the police station making a statement.

Now, alone in the silence of the private hospital room, Dylan struggled to believe this reality. His mind played over every moment since Dad had died as he tried to pinpoint where things had gone so wrong for Jack. Was he to blame for the choices his brother took that led him to this moment? Could he have been a better brother? Could he have paid more attention—

"Knock knock?"

The door creaked open behind him, and Dylan looked over his shoulder to see Dave's head poking around the door. "Come in, Dave," Dylan said, his voice flat.

"How's he doing?"

Dylan sat back in the hard hospital chair and sighed. "They tell me he's critical. He overdosed on a drug or a cocktail of drugs—they're not sure yet. They've taken blood and urine samples and will know more when the results come back."

"He's lucky you went looking for him."

"He won't agree, I can promise you that."

"No. Not immediately, but he will in time." Dave moved around to the other side of Jack's bed and pulled up a seat.

Dylan looked over the bed at Dave. His kind face and peaceful manner was like a breath of fresh air, and Dylan couldn't have wished for a better visitor at this point in time. "Thanks for coming in."

Dave shrugged and smiled an encouraging smile. "Everything will be ok. Trust that God has this all under control, and nothing has happened that He didn't allow."

"With all due respect, I don't think this is what God wanted," Dylan said.

"Not what God wanted, but what God allowed. What are the chances that you found what you needed to find the same night Jack overdosed? Fate? No. You were led to find that clue, which led to finding Jack, and which has ended up with him here in hospital, getting the best care he could get. Otherwise, the likelihood is he would have died at that party and no one would have noticed until it was too late."

"I know," Dylan said past the lump in his throat. The idea his little brother be dying on a dirty floor with no one around to help him, hurt. Physically hurt.

"You may not understand why God allowed this to happen, but you can rest in the fact that it is for your good and His glory," Dave said.

"My good?" Dylan asked, an eyebrow raised.

"Of course."

Dylan made a sound of disbelief and rubbed his temples. "I don't get that. Jack's issues have been disrupting my life for years, and he doesn't care. I've had the biggest opportunity given to me this year and Jack's thrown the biggest curveball ever. I don't see at all how any of this is for my good."

The door creaked open, and Dylan looked over his shoulder to see Nick and Trent entering. Nick gave him nod.

"Sorry to disturb you, but thought you might want to see what's on TV."

Dylan shrugged. Nick approached Jack's bedside table and collected the TV remote to turn on the TV unit hanging from the ceiling. The nightly news channel reporter filled the silence with some grim report, then the feed went live to a reporter standing in the foyer of this hospital. Dylan leaned forward.

"...Yes, thanks, Madeline. I'm here at the Winchester Parade Hospital, where just under an hour ago, the brother of rising AFL rising star Dylan Saunders was brought in after overdosing at a local party. Doctors cannot comment what drug or drugs were used, but have commented that the boy's condition is critical. It was approximately ten fifty-eight tonight that police responded to a triple-zero call from the site of a party. Upon arriving, police uncovered a vast quantity of illicit drugs and pornographic material believed to have a street value of just over two point five million dollars. A number of partygoers have been taken into custody. However, it is believed the main suspects fled the scene. Police are calling for anyone with information to come forward as—"

The room plunged into silence as Dylan switched off the TV and tossed the remote back onto Jack's nightstand. He closed his eyes and ground his teeth in an attempt to fight off the intense anger bubbling within him, shrugging off the hand that lightly fell upon his shoulder. He leaned forward and put his face in his hands. "I can't believe this. I cannot … believe this!"

Thankful no one tried to speak or put another hand on him, Dylan focused on his breathing and tried to stop his teeth grinding. He'd never been so mad. He had to get out of the room. He stood abruptly. "I gotta get out of here."

Without a look back at his friends, Dylan ripped the door open and strode out into the hall. He looked left and right, trying to orientate himself. He had no idea even what level he was on. He'd just followed Jack's bed until he was wheeled into the room he was now in. A nurse came into view, and Dylan hurried to her. "Excuse me."

"Yes?" she asked, her manner calm and polite.

"Can you tell me if there's a cafeteria around here?"

Her instructions were clear. Not five minutes later, Dylan was blowing the steam off a cup of hot chocolate from the café's vending machine. The vast room was empty. Just a sea of white chairs and tables before him and the soft hum of the TV speaking to itself in the corner.

"Sure you should be drinking that?" Dave's voice echoed quietly in the room.

Dylan closed his eyes and shook his head. "Nope. But my career is most likely over anyway, so who cares."

A chair pulled up beside him and Dylan opened his eyes to look at Dave. The man smiled back, humor glinting in his eyes. "I left Trent and Nick with your brother. I think we might need to have that chat now."

Dylan frowned. "What chat?"

"The chat we were going to have when you came to my place to resign from the leadership team, but it wasn't a good time for either of us to get into it then?"

The memory came back. He sipped the hot chocolate. "What do you want to talk about?"

"For the sake of time, I'm going to cut to the chase." Dave leaned forward in his seat. "Why do you think God called you to the leadership team?"

"I dunno. To be a leader, I guess," Dylan mumbled into his drink and took another sip, uncomfortable under Dave's intense gaze. Dave didn't respond. When the silence continued, he looked at Dave again and frowned. "What? You don't agree?"

"You really think you're a leader?" Dave sat back in his chair and crossed his arms.

Sensing a challenge, Dylan chuckled. "I think that's pretty obvious."

"Interesting," Dave said. "You see, I believe you are an encourager. Matter-of-fact, that's what your friend's say too."

"An encourager?" Dylan said the word like it tasted bad in his mouth. "You may as well say I'm the weak one."

"No. Dylan." Dave leaned forward and put a hand on Dylan's shoulder. "An encourager is the heart. The inner strength. The safe house when everything is falling down. There are many encouragers in the Bible who helped the leaders be who they were and do what they did—Aaron, Jonathan, Caleb, to name a few. We need encouragers."

Dylan shook his head and finished the hot chocolate. "I don't see it that way, Dave. I'm a leader. Always have been." He punctuated his sentence by tossing the cup in the bin, then looked back at Dave. The older man looked back at him like a father might, with patience and understanding in his eyes.

"Look at what you helped the Tigers accomplish since you joined their team," Dave said. "You've ensured your mum didn't break down completely after your Dad passed. You helped Lexi get through a difficult time—and wasn't it your suggestion to do the encouragement cards that night we managed to get her back to youth?"

Dave took a quick look at his watch, then rose. "Dylan, I could go on. I've known you for a long time but, this is a matter between you and God. Pray about it and see where it leads, but I can tell you one thing: encouragers are not weak. They're the furthest thing from it. In the meantime, trust that God will send a leader when the time is right."

# FORTY-SIX

Dylan watched the sun rise from the porch swing of his family's home illuminating the countryside in warming rays of yellow, orange, and red. Unable to sleep when he came home from the hospital, he'd gone outside to try and clear his mind. What Dave had said to him last night had struck a chord and he couldn't stop thinking about it.

All those things he said … wasn't that just good leadership?

The cockatoos, magpies, and corellas took flight, filling the early silence with their calls. Dylan rubbed his face and sighed, soul weary and despondent. He could feel a war within himself: career or family. As the sun brightened the land around him, it dawned that he couldn't have both. He was going to have to choose.

And no matter how he cut it, his family would always come first.

His stomach rumbled and he considered getting up to make breakfast, but he couldn't motivate his limbs to move him to the kitchen. He sighed again. How could a year that promised so much wind up to be so disappointing?

The screen door opened behind him. He turned to see Mum stepping out onto the verandah and take a deep breath of the morning breeze. She looked as if she hadn't slept a wink either. "Morning, Mum."

She started and gripped the railing as she looked over at him. "Sweetie. I thought you were still in bed."

"Didn't sleep," Dylan said, rubbing his eyes.

"Me either."

She moved towards him with stiff measured steps and slowly sank into the porch swing beside him, pulling her dressing gown snug around her body. "Thank you so much for going out after him."

Dylan took in her unblinking stare as she looked out over the countryside, and the reddening flush moving over her face. Was she about to burst into tears or—

"I don't know what I'd do without you." Her voice caught and she turned to him. When her reddened eyes met his and she grasped his hand, Dylan felt moments from embarrassing himself. He cleared his throat. "Mum. You never have to worry about that."

"I know you've got your big career going and we hold you back. I saw the news last night …"

Dylan acknowledged the comment about the news and looked back over the view. The neighbors' horses were enjoying playing with each other, and it brought a smile to his face. What she said was true, and he didn't need reminding of the news report last night. He blew his breath out. What he needed was food. "Want me to make you something for breakfast?"

"No, thanks. I'm not hungry."

Ten minutes later, Dylan was sitting at the table looking at a plate full of scrambled eggs, grilled tomatoes, and toast. He was about to take his first bite when the screen door banged shut and Mum flashed past the open doorway of the kitchen. He got to his feet. "Mum?"

"Someone's here!" she yelled from the rear of the house before slamming the bathroom door. Dylan grinned. No matter how down Mum was, she still took pride in her appearance when going out or when people came around. He walked to the front and pushed through the screen door. A scarlet red Lamborghini had pulled up in the driveway. That was unexpected. Dylan was still wearing his rumbled jeans and T-shirt from last night. He ran his hands over his hair, hoping he was presentable enough to whoever showed themselves. Lachlan appeared from behind the tinted windows as he stepped out of the car, and Dylan felt his eyebrows rise. What was he doing here?

"Good morning, Mr. Ward." Dylan stepped down from the verandah towards him. Lachlan offered his hand, his smile warm. "Lachlan, please son."

"Lachlan." Dylan corrected himself. It still felt strange to call someone of authority by their first name, since his dad had taught him to greet people with respect. "Sorry, again. Old habits die hard. What brings you all the way out to The Valley?"

achlan about
cupied with
m in the first place?

ould
. mann

on the door as Dave's
er of hope appeared.
new it, and nothing
, as he stood in the
before him in the
was going to bring
ded to ride, to bring
Nick's. As soon as
ved, Dylan made

happy laughter
s to head back
e last time he'd
inting to hold
ne black cloud
ed the screen
be willing to
e," he whis-
een door.
ding disap-
seated and
d chuckled. Should he go inside? This
adn't seen coming.

if I come in?"
Dylan cleared his
1. Please come in."
a stepped out onto
d up loosely with a
a smile he'd not seen
r visitor joining us for

nodded. "Yep.

n to introduce him, but
od on the verandah look-
Before Dylan could put a
uared his shoulders, put on
de towards the house. "Good
dent of the Condors Football

shook Lachlan's hand; was

eyebrows rose while he watched
de, the sound of easy laughter fol-
osed behind them. Dylan plunged his

at down.
to table

he did need to speak with L

ntract, his thoughts were more o

ought Lachlan all the way out to visit h

*God will send a leader in His time.*

Dylan straightened. His eyes narrowed

words echoed through his mind. A glimm

The Bible said God causes all things to w

good and His glory, and Dylan knew it. He

would move his conviction on that fact. But

quiet of the morning having nothing certai

more, he couldn't make sense of how God v

this mess around into something good. He nee

through his thoughts. But his bike was still at

Lachlan had gone, he'd get his bike back. Reso

his way inside.

The sounds of animated conversation and

enveloped Dylan as he climbed the verandah ste

inside. He paused at the threshold. When was th

heard Mum laugh? An uncomfortable mix of wa

onto the memories of his dad and wanting to see t

that had been over the family gone, Dylan gripp

door handle. For that black cloud to go, he had to

see it go. He sucked in a deep breath. "Jesus, help n

pered as he let his breath out and pulled open the sc

As soon as Dylan entered the kitchen, any forebo

peared. There was three mugs on the table, mum was

Lachlan was perusing a cupboard.

"Where's your sugar, Jenny?"

Mum got up to help make the drinks as Dylan

Lachlan took the sugar off Mum, then ushered her back

to sit. The man oozed confidence, even in situations he wasn't sure about. The tinkling of a teaspoon against ceramic soon filled the room.

"Dylan, I hope you don't mind, but since your breakfast had gone cold, I fixed you another plate."

Dylan chuckled. "I could have eaten it cold."

"I did tell him that, but he insisted." Mum's eyes sparkled, and Dylan sat back in his seat as a mug with curls of steam rising from its rim was placed in front of him. "What are we drinking, boss?"

Lachlan collected a plate of the bench, and returned to the table and placed it in front of Dylan, then sat at the table to join them. "Considering the night you've had, strong coffee."

Dylan dipped his head in thanks. He didn't drink coffee, let alone strong coffee, but he was feeling like a wrung-out mop so would gratefully accept any form of hospitality. The smell of scrambled eggs filled his senses, and he remembered his hunger. Without a second thought, Dylan dug in.

"There was another reason I wanted to see you both." Lachlan settled back into his seat and crossed his arms.

Mum sipped at her drink. "What was that?"

"Before I became the president of the Condors Football Club, my background was law ..."

Dylan looked up from his plate and fixed his eyes on Lachlan. The man knew something he didn't, and it was hidden in what he wasn't saying.

Jack was in serious trouble.

# FORTY-SEVEN

"Here she is mate, just as you left her."

As Nick pulled the garage door up and Dylan saw his bike again, he couldn't help but smile. He was thankful for the use of his mum's car, but there was something about the bike. "Nick. Brother. I owe you."

With a few steps, Dylan crossed the garage floor and climbed onto his bike. It felt like home—the smell of leather and chrome, the feeling of it settling into its suspension under his weight, the hand grips in his grasp. "Seriously, if Jack had got his hands on this bike, I don't know what I'd have done to him."

Nick grinned humorlessly. "How is he?"

"He's awake. Cops are guarding his door, and he faces a string of charges."

"I suspected as much. Are they sending him to rehab first?"

Dylan sniffed. "He has to undergo a court assessment order first to determine what sentence gets handed down." He looked up at Nick. "How much time could he be looking at for charges of procession and dealing in drugs, robbery, aggravated assault, and sex with a minor?"

"Depends." Nick stepped into the garage, rested a hip against the wall, and crossed his arms. "Was he caught with a minor?"

"I caught him. Although he claims she's of age."

"I mean, has she made a statement or are they in a relationship?"

"I checked Jack's phone. She's going to report him."

Nick grimaced. "It depends on her age, but yeah, it'll get messy. I can tell you that much."

Dylan mm'd. "My boss came out this morning. Turns out he has a background in law."

"He could be a very handy ace to have up your sleeve." Nick looked impressed and Dylan sat back on his bike and crossed his arms. Dave's words flashed back into his mind again and the sensation of carrying a load eased. "As much as Jack is a pain in the butt, I'd never wish what he's got coming on anyone. And what makes it worse, I don't know what I can do to help."

"We are all a product of our own decisions, mate. Nobody can make you do anything. Don't beat yourself up for things he's chosen to do," Nick said.

While Dylan knew his friend was right, he still couldn't shake the feeling that if he'd been around a bit more then Jack might not have ended up as lost as he was. He needed time to think. With a dip of his head, Dylan laid a few quick raps on Nick's chest before starting the bike. Nothing needed to be said. Nick lifted his hand in a wave as Dylan drove the bike out of the garage.

The open road was just what he needed. Time on his own to think and—if God was still listening to him—to pray. Once clear of town, Dylan laid on the throttle and opened the bike up until it screamed beneath him. Finally, he could release the frustration that had been building inside him. Behind the helmet and blackened visor, nobody would recognize him. As the turn off he wanted approached, he dropped the gears, enjoying the roar of the bike, and veered off to the left to take the scenic route to Red Bluff lookout.

Through the air vents of the visor, Dylan picked up the sweet scent of eucalyptus from the towering gum trees and the musty understory around him as he climbed the mountain towards the lookout. The peaceful scenery and relaxing ride soothed his mind, but he knew the relief was only temporary.

"God," Dylan said behind his helmet. "I don't understand why all this is happening. You promised that if we follow you, you'll give us the desires of our hearts. I do follow you. I go to church and help others to follow you and I was sure you'd given me what I wanted, only to find it gets ripped from my hands. Not that it's been ripped from my hands, but you know. The writing is on the wall. I have to give up football to look after my stupid brother who can't look after himself and thinks its ok to abuse himself, Mum, and underage girls. Where'd he get that from? He made his decisions and I made mine, so why are his constantly affecting me?"

You're the one who set me up, Lord. You're the one who gave me the skills and the opportunity. I didn't go looking for a career with the AFL. But I accepted it and even got to witness for you to a few of the fellas at the club. C'mon, I'm doing your will. I don't get at all why you'd give this to me then—"

He fell silent. He didn't recognize his own voice or the things he was saying. He felt the rebuke within his mind as the First Commandment echoed loudly inside his mind: 'Thou shalt not have any other gods before me.'

Dylan turned off to the lookout and pulled his bike up at the edge and looked out over the expanse of cerulean blue ocean. Had he put football before God? A flashback from training camp came to mind, a flashback of Tom telling him to pull his head in. He grimaced. With a heavy sigh, he pulled the helmet off and rested it on the handlebars as Trent's words came into his mind: 'Pride comes before the fall.'

The wind rustled in the tree canopy above him, and he looked up. Never had he felt so small or embarrassed. He rubbed his eyes and Lexi's accusation come back to mind: 'I think football is becoming more than just a game to you.' He groaned under the weight of his conscience. She was right, and he'd bitten her head off. A lump formed in his throat and his chest seemed to implode on itself. How was it that he'd lost himself and not known?

He took a deep breath, trying to release the pressure on his chest but it wouldn't release. He yawned, he paced, he coughed. The discomfort remained, and he rubbed a fist up and down his sternum. How had he not seen what was happening or how his priorities were changing? Since when did a game become more important than his family? Since when had he become so prideful? Angry at himself, he kicked the gravel beneath his feet and looked out over the water. There was so much to make right, but where did he start? Running his hands over his hair, he slumped back against the bike and bowed his head, his arms falling limply at his sides. "God, I'm so sorry. What do I do?"

As he spoke, his phone vibrated in the bike's saddlebag. Uninterested, he nevertheless dug the phone out to check the message.

*'Come back to Leadership Team? Dave.'*

The wind picked up, stirring up the leaves around him, and he watched as they scuttled off the side of the lookout and floated lazily on the breeze down towards the water. As he took in the awesome grandeur of the ocean, a light sensation tickled his skin. The corner of his mouth hitched up.

"Ok, God. I'll start there."

# FORTY-EIGHT

Dylan paused at the door of Dave's house, his knuckles resting against the leadlight panel, ready to knock.

Should he or shouldn't he? He hadn't answered Dave's text yesterday, so nobody would know if he turned and left. He chuckled. This was crazy. Not six months ago, this had been one of his favorite places. Just as went to knock, the door opened from the inside.

"Dave!" Dylan withdrew his arm.

"Well, are you coming in?" Dave asked.

Dylan coughed as he pocked his hands. "I was just about to knock, actually."

Dave stepped back and opened the door. "We've been waiting for you. Everyone's in the library."

"Hang on, how did you know I was here?" Dylan asked, stepping over the threshold.

"The same reason why I messaged you, asking for you to come back. God wants you here. I knew you'd come."

Dylan chuckled, unable to deny Dave's logic. He was uncharacteristically nervous, and he massaged the nape of his neck as he followed Dave to the library. Just beyond those doors was a life he thought he'd left behind. Now he wasn't sure how he'd fit back in.

"Guys, looks who's joining us tonight," Dave said as he entered the room and gestured for him to follow. All unease vanished as soon as he caught sight of his friends' smiling faces looking back at him. He stepped into the room and closed the door behind him. Trent rose, extending a hand. "Brother, it's great to see you."

"Hey, Dylan!" Hope shuffled over on the couch. "Sit."

"Welcome back." Lexi straightened up in one of the tub chairs in front of Dave's desk. Nick got up from the pew in front of the window and crossed the room towards him. He extended his hand and Dylan shook it. "Good to see you back. The kids have been asking after you. They're going to be stoked to see you back on deck."

Not wanting to encourage Hope, Dylan chose to sit next to Nick. As Dave called the meeting to order, Dylan took a moment to look over the room. Everything was the same. Had he even been gone? Time had flown so fast it was hard to imagine so much had happened since the last time he'd sat in this library and co—

"Dylan, what do you think?"

He blinked. Everyone was looking at him, encouraging smiles on their faces. He coughed into a fist. "Sorry, Dave, I was lost in thought. What was the question?"

Dave chuckled. "We have someone bust in on our Youth night acting dunk, looking shabby, swinging a bottle etcetera. I'm looking to see how the young people will react. Would they look to us? Or would they reach out and try to help the 'distressed' person? What do you think?"

Dylan leaned forward and linked his hands between his knees. "Sounds great, Dave. Are you worried about if it frightens some of the younger kids? What is the lesson in the end?"

Nick gave Dylan a horse bite on his thigh and Dylan responded with a playful punch to Nick's upper arm. "What was that for?"

"For not paying attention." Nick laughed.

"It's ok, Dylan. Nick's going to escort the guy out once the point has been made." Hope said, tucking her hair behind her ears.

"The overall point is, do you love your neighbor?" Lexi said. "But it's important to realize there could be some teens who aren't happy about being tricked."

Dave shuffled his notes on the table then laid them to the side in a neat pile. "That is where you guys come in. We break off into small group studies afterwards, with each of you leading a group. I've written out a list of discussion questions." Dave handed papers over the table to Lexi, who handed them out.

Dylan tried to catch her eye when she offered him a paper, but she kept her eyes shuttered as she looked over him to Nick. While he was relieved to have been welcomed back into the leadership team, there was still tension between himself and Lexi. He looked over the list of questions in his hand, pretending to read them while he considered how to reconcile with one of his best friends. Movement in the room drew his attention. Lexi and Hope stood as if ready to leave.

"Yep, I'll bring the supper this week," Hope said to Dave.

"And I'll turn up early to help set up." Lexi made a note on the paper in front of her before looking over at Hope. "Are you still ok to take me home tonight?"

Dylan could sense an opportunity arise to intercede when Hope's face warped to worry and she turned to Lexi. "Oh sorry hun, I completely forgot -

"You up for drinks tonight?" Nick said, folding his own papers and pocketing them.

Nick's voice interrupted his concentration on the conversation he was trying to listen in on, and he glanced over at him. "Ah, yeah, sure. Where?"

"Bye, guys. See you all on Friday night." Hope moved to the door.

"I was thinking the usual place. The Beachside," Nick said.

The room echoed with goodbyes. Lexi and Trent exchanged a few words which ended with Lexi's expression changing to relief. He turned to Nick. "Hold on a second, will you."

Without waiting for Nick to respond, Dylan rose and stepped around the coffee table to Lexi's side.

"I was just about to come say goodbye to you guys," she said.

"Yeah. Hey, ah, I overheard you were after a lift home?" His words were oddly difficult to get out.

She brushed the fringe from her eyes as color filled her cheeks, "Trent's already offered, so…"

Dylan took a step back, feeling like the elephant in the room. "Sure, no worries."

"See you Friday night, then?" Lexi's smile was bright as she stepped around him and moved towards the door, but he sensed she was uncomfortable around him by the way she hugged her notepad against her chest. They'd not been in such close quarters since the afternoon when she'd bailed him up about his family. He still remembered the darkness in her eyes and the shake of her hand on the verandah railing as she left. He flashed a grin.

"I'll be there."

# FORTY-NINE

"Do you really want to do this, son?" Lachlan asked, his fingers steepled as he watched Dylan closely over his desk.

"Yes, I do," Dylan replied, his tone matter-of-fact as he stared down Lachlan's piercing, perceptive gaze. He would not be talked out of the decision he'd come all this way to carry out. This afternoon, he would leave the Condors headquarters for the last time. From there, only God knew.

Lachlan stood and moved to the large window behind his desk, overlooking the city. His broad shoulders silhouetted against the afternoon sun made him appear even more imposing. "Well, Dylan, I have to say that saddens me. You have incredible potential." He turned. "I admire you for putting your family first. However, would you be open to taking a leave of absence on com-

Dylan pushed through the double entry glass doors of the Condor team headquarters and out into the afternoon sun. A sense of peace and release settled over him and he looked skyward. The cloudless cerulean sky held his gaze for longer than a moment. What was God's plan was for him now? He'd be so sure it was joining the Condors, but the once-glittering future he'd held in the palm of his hand now lay scattered at his feet like a house of cards blown over in the wind.

With a sigh he tore his gaze back to earth and headed towards his bike. At least there was a silver lining. Lachlan was a good man, and God knew he needed help around the place. Jack was in serious trouble and Mum's sanity had been hanging on by a thread. Perhaps his time with the Condors was so he could meet Lachlan, so Lachlan could meet Mum.

If that was the reason, then what about Jack? What was his silver lining? If anything, Jack's current reality would drive him further from God.

With a growl, Dylan kicked his bike into life and thundered towards the highway. He wove through the mounting late afternoon traffic, considering how he might try to put the pieces of his old life back together.

But was that what God wanted for him? He had no idea. Only time would tell. But in the Bible stories he'd listened to when he was growing up, the people acted first out of faith, then God moved. So he would move in the direction he wanted and trust the outcome to God. With that, he steered the bike into the left-hand lane to take the next turn.

To see Lexi.

# FIFTY

It was nearing five-thirty by the time Dylan reached Lexi's place. He had hoped to get to her place sooner, but he'd swung by home to grab an extra helmet – if things went to plan. But now, it was getting close to dinner time. It would be best to keep riding. But he didn't want to. He didn't want another night wondering whether he'd lost his chance with Lexi. Worst-case scenario, wondering if he'd lost her friendship. If he could have part of the mess he'd made cleared up by nightfall, he would.

When Dylan pulled up, Shaun was in the driveway with a friend, a basketball tucked under his arm. Dylan pulled off his helmet and dipped his head. "Evening, fellas."

"Hey." Shaun gestured to his friend and he introduced them. "Dylan, this is Troy. Troy, this is Dylan."

"Nice bike!" Troy said, his eyes the size of dinner plates as he looked over Dylan's motorbike before turning back towards Shaun. "Is this the bloke who—"

Shaun laughed and thrust the basketball into Troy's stomach, drawing a grunt from the man as he stumbled back. "Lexi's inside," Shaun said. "And sorry to hear about your brother. Tough break, man."

Dylan looked between Shaun and Troy, who now had an impish grin on his face while spinning the basketball on a fingertip. He nodded. Tough break was an understatement. He turned his gaze back to Shaun. "It's going to be a long hard road back for him, but I'm sure he'll be right. You boys looking to have a good season?"

"We have a solid team. Just got to work on shots from outside the key, as we don't have the height that other teams have."

Tired of small talk and aware the day was fast drawing to a close, Dylan glanced towards the house. "All right, fellas. I better leave you to your practice."

"No worries." Shaun said backing up. "Go ahead. Just head on in."

Dylan turned to the house and frowned. What was that about? And who was Troy?

Lexi was outside in the garden, reading. She looked up as the door clicked open. He smiled and dipped his head. "Evening." Her spine straightened as he approached.

"Hey." Lexi swept her fringe from her eyes. "What brings you here?"

Dylan sat on the garden chair beside her. She pulled the book to her chest and toyed with the corners. Her tension was palpable.

"Did you see Troy in the driveway?"

Dylan let his breath out on a chuckle, thankful for a chance at levity. "Yeah. What's with that guy?"

"Oh, he's a bit of a fan …" The corner of her mouth hitched up and Dylan's eyes narrowed.

"A fan of what? Football?" He asked. Where was she leading with a comment like that?

She grinned and reached for her bottle of water. "Let's just say … Troy didn't like Brad either, so when he heard you'd knocked Brad into next week? Well, he's wanted to meet you ever since."

Dylan rubbed a hand over his hair, unsure if he wanted followers because of a car park skirmish. "I wouldn't say I knocked him into next week," Dylan said quietly. "I just gave him the old 'don't argue'."

Lexi grinned and Dylan knew she didn't believe him. "Dylan, I saw your knuckles. You gave him more than an open-palm shove."

Dylan straightened, impressed. "How do you know what a 'don't argue' is?"

"How long have we been friends?" Lexi asked, eyebrow raised. "I do listen when you talk football."

Dylan grinned back at her. The tension had dropped away, and his friend was back. His plan flashed into his mind. As the silence lengthened, he blurted it out before the moment could be lost.

"Wanna come for a ride?"

Lexi blinked. "On your bike?"

He loved the color pooling into her cheeks. "Yeah."

Lexi looked away as she shifted on the garden chair. Dylan knew she'd be weighing up the possible reasons for him asking her to come out for a ride, and he hoped she'd say yes. Or would she been too nervous? The rapid pulse jumping in her throat suggested the latter.

"Where to?" Lexi turned worried eyes back to him.

Dylan wanted her to relax. Was it him, or was it the idea of being on the back of a motorbike that had her keyed up? He suspected both. "Just to Red Bluff Lookout. I'll go slow. No shenanigans. You'll be safe. I promise."

A whisper of a grin tickled her mouth, though she still held her book in a death grip. "Ok. Um. When?"

Dylan suppressed his elation and rose to his feet. Lexi's eyes widened as she looked up at him. "What, now?" she asked.

Dylan handed the helmet in his hands over to her.

"Yeah. Now."

# FIFTY-ONE

"Dylan, this place is amazing!" Lexi's words were muffled by her helmet.

A grin tipped the corner of Dylan's mouth as he pulled the helmet off his head. "Well, better jump off and enjoy the view while we still have some sunlight."

She wasted no time. She'd removed her helmet and alighted the bike before Dylan had unzipped his jacket. He swung a leg over the bike and relaxed back against it, watching Lexi approach the lookout platform. He found the view of the town below them calming. The ocean stretched out as far as the eye could see, the streetlights and house lights dotting the landscape like fairy lights, all bathed in a golden glow from the setting sun. The vista was breathtaking, just like the view of young woman standing before him.

As if sensing his gaze, Lexi turned. "How are you? Feels like we haven't spoken in ages."

"That's because it's been ages." Dylan took his riding gloves off.

She nodded slowly, her face reflecting the myriad thoughts going through her mind. Dylan laid the gloves over the handlebars and crossed his arms. He'd love to know what she was thinking right about now.

"I heard about your brother," Lexi said eventually.

Dylan cleared his throat. This was not the conversation he was hoping for. "Yeah."

"How is he doing?"

"Well, there is a whole lot of reality waiting for him when he's well enough to face it." Dylan said. "A part of me is happy it's happened. Another part is annoyed at myself for not being around more to try and prevent it." He looked away from Lexi's gaze, frustration rising again. Prayers to feel more love for his brother flooded his mind and he rubbed his forehead. Perhaps God would answer his prayer in time, but as of this moment, He hadn't.

"You ok?"

Lexi's voice was close, and he looked up, struck by her nearness and the look of compassion in her eyes, he dropped his guard. "Not really. My brother is facing jail, I have no job and—"

"You have no job?" Lexi's hand brushed his arm, leaving trail of warmth in its wake.

Dylan sighed. "Well, not exactly. I've decided to take a leave of absence from the club until family things are sorted out. I went to speak with my boss this morning. I actually went there to quit altogether, but he's a good negotiator." A whisper of a smile tugged at Dylan's mouth. He liked Lachlan. "Anyway, I think I need to be around home more often, and Matt doesn't need me at the garage since he hired someone else."

"Wow." Lexi breathed as she moved to lean against the bike next to him. "Wow. Dylan, I had no idea. I feel awful."

He turned to look at her. "Why do you feel awful?"

"Well, I should have been there to support you, but what did I do? Instead, I turn up at your house and yell at you."

Dylan breathed a soft chuckle. "Ah, yeah, about that. I was the one who asked Mum to talk to you, so she wouldn't talk to everyone else about what was happening with Jack."

Lexi's eyes widened and she slapped his arm. "Why didn't you tell me? Now I feel stupid."

"I was under strict instructions from Nick. But I did think about telling you." Dylan said, bumping her knee with his.

The sun was melting into the horizon, casting long shadows around them, and the temperature had dropped. It would be dark soon, but he didn't want to leave. He was enjoying Lexi's company without the awkwardness that had been between them for so many months. The moment lengthened, and Lexi looked back at him, a blush forming on her cheeks. His chest tightened. Was this the moment to tell her what he felt for her, or—

She looked away.

A deep ache penetrated his heart as he took in her quiet profile a moment longer, then dropped his gaze. Friends it was, it seemed. He should be happy. At least that was something. At least he hadn't lost her completely. So why did it feel like he had? He sighed and scratched the stubble on his chin at the thought, at the weight on his heart and in his mind.

"I've made a mess of everything, haven't I?" Dylan stared at the ground between his riding boots, his voice subdued. "I've lost opportunities and hurt people I care about. And for what? Nothing." Resigned, he zipped up his jacket and reached for his gloves. "Come on. I better get you home."

"Wait." Lexi reached for his thigh, her voice as soft as her touch, and a surge of longing engulfed Dylan. He turned to her and felt his body respond as the heat from where her hand lay burned. She was so close that he could see the last of the sun slip beneath the horizon reflected in her eyes.

"Not for nothing." Lexi moistened her lips and her throat worked. "Remember Jeremiah 29:11?"

There was a catch in her voice, and Dylan felt a tremor in her body. As she moistened her lips again, his gaze dropped to her mouth, enticing in its nearness and glistening from each nervous run of her tongue. His resolve broke down and he kissed her.

Her breath hitched as his lips brushed against hers, electrifying every inch of his body, but Dylan resisted the urge to deepen his kiss. Instead, he drank in the moment that he had been desiring for so long. The warmth of her touch, her subtle scent of vanilla and the taste of her strawberry lip balm, swept over him taking time away with it. His head began to swim. It was Lexi's lips against his, Lexi kissing him back. He cupped the nape of her neck and wove his fingers into her silken hair holding her to him before he felt her hand press against his chest. The signal was weak, but he reined himself in and pulled back.

"I thought you promised no shenanigans." Lexi's hand on his chest now clung, rather than pushing.

"I meant while on the bike," Dylan whispered. His voice roughened as he collected her hand off his chest and pressed a kiss to her palm. Lexi's breath was uneven through her parted lips, as his fingers traced the skin on the back on her neck. He'd never seen her eyes so dark. He leaned in once more.

"We're still on the bike." Lexi said softly against his lips, her voice shaking.

Dylan paused, a grin playing on his mouth. He dropped his head, letting his breath out. She was right. He rested his forehead against hers and took another long breath, then let it out. She was intoxicating, a heady mix of sass and class. "I've really missed you, Lex."

Lexi sighed heavily. "I've missed you too."

Dylan looked up. Though dark was setting in fast, he could see a whisper of a smile on her face as she looked back at him. "I thought I'd lost you." Letting his hand slip from the back of her neck, he collected her hand from his thigh, and entwined his fingers with hers. "Not sure what I would have done if that happened."

"I'm not going anywhere," Lexi whispered as a cool breeze swept up the understory around them. For the first time in months, he felt peaceful. Relaxed, he turned from her to look out over the darkening view. A thread of amber lined the horizon, highlighting where sky and ocean met, while the sounds of nightlife geared up below. He didn't want to leave.

"I know that verse you said before," Dylan said quietly, looking down to where their hands were knotted together on his lap. "I get that God has a plan for each of us that is for our own good. I just don't see it in my case. At this point in time, I guess."

"That's where faith comes in, Dylan." Lexi rubbed her thumb over the back of his hand, her voice steady. He looked from where their hands were to her face. If anyone understood faith when nothing made sense, it was Lexi. His eyes travelled her face as he recalled what she'd been through.

"What is it?" Lexi gazed back at him, her eyes searching.

A whisper of a smile turned up the corners of Dylan's mouth. Captivated by the way her eyes seemed to sparkle like the stars above, he gave a slight shake of his head. "Nothing." Lexi dropped her head, but not before Dylan noticed her catch her bottom lip between her teeth. He tipped her chin back to him. She moistened her lips and he found himself drawn to her again.

The car park lights flickered on, bathing them in their dull tawny light, and Dylan pulled back reluctantly. "I need to get you back home." His voice tremulous as he ran the back of his knuckles down her cheek, then trailing his thumb along her lower lip. Her mouth parted at his touch and the warmth of her breath on his fingers sent a thrill up his spine. He closed his eyes. They had to go. He pushed himself off the bike, and snagged his helmet and gloves, then he looked back at Lexi. She was still leaning against the bike with a faraway look on her face.

"You ok, Lex?" Dylan asked.

She raised her eyes to him and exhaled a soft laugh. "Uh, yeah I think so. I'm just not sure I trust my legs."

Dylan chuckled and pulled on his helmet, needing a barrier between them. "Need a hand?" He fastened the clip under his chin. Lexi continued to smile that dreamy, contented grin at him before she blinked a number of times and looked around.

"No. I'll be right."

With a grace Dylan wasn't expecting in the wake of her confession, Lexi moved off the bike, pulled on her helmet, and climbed onto the pillion cushion. When she turned to him, Dylan pulled the straps of his gloves tight and in one fluid motion alighted the bike. As the roar of the Harley coming to life echoed off the quiet of the evening, Dylan flicked his visor down and turned the bike out of the lookout car-park.

The roads were clear. While he knew he had to get Lexi home out of respect to her parents, he didn't want to rush. So he chose to coast the bike lazily down the mountainside, loving the feel of Lexi wrapped around him and his clear conscience. Though still annoyed with himself for falling so easily to pride, that wasn't something he'd ever do again. He made a promise to God. God would come first. He would live his faith and practice his belief, no matter if it went against what he wanted.

As he pulled up at a crossroad and waited for traffic to pass, he took a moment to look skyward. What he wanted, was direction.

"God," Dylan murmured behind his helmet. "What do I do now? Where do you want me?"

A shooting star grabbed his attention and as his eyes travelled the skies with it, his mind suddenly cleared. A clear impression came to him and he smiled.

*"Follow me."*

# SHORT BIBLE STUDY: DYLAN

1.    Was it a coincidence Dylan's coach called him to talk about the Condors just as Dylan had declared his desire to help others in Chapter Six?

_____

_____

_____

_____

_____

_____

_____

2.    Which offer do you think God intended for Dylan, the Tigers or the Condors? Why?

_____

_____

_____

_____

_____

_____

3.    How was Dylan's prayer answered in Chapter Thirty-Six?

_____

_____

_____

_____

_____

_____

_____

4. What did Dave mean when he described Encouragers as "the heart. The inner strength. The safe house when everything is falling down."? Who encourages you and what do they mean to you?

_____

_____

_____

_____

_____

_____

_____

5. Dylan prayed a lot over his family. Can you list the ways you believe God answered those prayers? Do you see God answering prayers in your life?

_____

_____

_____

_____

_____

_____

_____

# ABOUT THE AUTHOR

K.J. Rowe began her writing career in 2012 with the drafting of her Young Adult series called "Casts of Silver", The series, born out of her own unique experiences and understanding how books can literally change people's lives has been crafted to spotlight particular issues common amongst young people. To impress upon youth the importance of listening to their inner voice, remembering their self worth and to trust in Gods perfect plan for each of our lives is the mission and vision of this series. Karen lives with her husband and 2 children on a farm in North West Victoria, Australia.